To Sharon

Merry Christmas!

The Christmas Collection

Victoria Connelly

with very best wishes

Victoria Connelly

No part of this publication may be reproduced, distributed, or transmitted in any form or by any means, including photocopying, recording, or other electronic or mechanical methods, without the prior written permission of the publisher.

The characters and events portrayed in this book are fictitious. Any resemblance to actual persons, living or dead, is entirely coincidental.

Victoria Connelly asserts the moral right to be identified as the author of this work.

Cover design by J D Smith.

The Christmas Collection is a compilation of the following titles:

Christmas at the Cove 2014
Christmas at the Castle 2015
Christmas at the Cottage 2016

Published by Cuthland Press
in association with Notting Hill Press.

Copyright © 2016 Victoria Connelly

All rights reserved.

ISBN: 978-1-910522-12-7

Christmas at the Cove

To Caroline Fardell with love.

CHAPTER 1

Millie Venning hadn't been looking forward to Christmas until she'd got a phone call from her Great Aunt Louise.

'Now, didn't you say you wanted to stay at the cottage sometime?' her aunt asked without any sort of preamble. 'Well, it's standing empty over Christmas.'

Millie had smiled as childhood memories of holidays at the cottage overlooking the little cove on the exposed north Devon coast flooded back to her – the big black rocks she'd scrambled over with her brothers, the acres of cool, damp sand and the wonderful wildness of it all. It was just what she needed to blow away the end of year office blues.

It would also be a blessing to get away from her flat in Bath. Although in a beautiful Georgian terrace overlooking a pretty garden filled with roses in the summer and holly berries in the winter, the flat itself had been converted with sound-proofing very low on the builder's list of priorities, and two of her neighbours had entered into the Christmas spirit already with parties lasting into the early hours.

So, the day before Christmas Eve, she packed her largest suitcase full of all her warmest jumpers, chucked a few essentials from her kitchen cupboards into a couple of carrier bags and prepared herself for the drive south, hoping that her old Citroen would make the journey. It had been making some decidedly odd noises and it was due for a service but she hadn't had the funds to take care of it – not on her salary and certainly not after the washing machine explosion which had flooded her kitchen and emptied her bank account as she'd sorted out the whole sorry mess.

She shook her head. She wasn't going to think of all that now nor was she going to think of her ex-boyfriend, James, whom she should have been spending the holidays with. They were meant to be jetting off to Morocco to spend Christmas in the sun – just the two of them. But …

Millie blinked away the tears that threatened to spill. She was *not* going to waste any more tears on him and yet, no matter how often she told herself that she was over him, her emotions would betray

1

her. It wasn't surprising really. After all, they'd been together for six years. She'd met him on the night of her thirtieth birthday party in a restaurant where her best friend, Trisha, had arranged a surprise party for her.

'This is the hottest spot in town for meeting people,' Trisha had told her and, sure enough, sometime between the main course and dessert, her eyes had met James's across the room.

She'd thought they'd be together forever but forever was a lot shorter these days, she couldn't help thinking. Forever was an outdated concept when it came to the men Millie had had the misfortune of meeting but she wouldn't want to be with someone like James forever, would she? Not when she'd discovered he'd been seeing a whole string of women behind her back. One would have been bad enough but four – or was it five – really was the limit.

If only she wasn't such a dreamer, she thought. But weren't most women? Didn't most women plan ahead once they thought they'd found the right man? Millie certainly had. She'd thought it was only a matter of time before she and James would get married and have children in that old-fashioned but rather wonderful order. She'd so longed for that and was beginning to get worried that it was too late for her. After all, she was thirty-six. Her daughter should have been learning to read by now and her son should have taken his first unsteady steps.

She shook her head, dispelling her fictionalised family from her mind.

'Perhaps fate has something else in store for you,' her Great Aunt Louise had said to her when Millie told her about her split with James.

'I'd like to know what,' Millie had said.

Good old Aunt Louise. Since her parents had moved to Canada over ten years ago, seventy-two year old Louise had taken it upon herself to become a surrogate mother to Millie, checking up on her with lengthy phone calls and popping round to her flat with fresh flowers and home-made pies and pastries. She lived in a little cottage on the outskirts of Bath, drove a car that was even older and more dilapidated than Millie's and was becoming more eccentric by the day but Millie adored her. Only her aunt hadn't been in the best of health lately. Millie had been worried, wondering if a care home was on the cards in the near future.

Aunt Louise had been so supportive since Millie's breakup with James too.

'Well, I can't say that I ever liked him much, anyway!' she'd said.

Millie had tried not to laugh, knowing that her aunt had fallen for his charms as much as she had.

'Someone *much* better is waiting just around the corner for you,' she'd told her great niece and she'd sounded so sure too. But how could she be?

Leaving the motorway at Taunton, Millie began the arduous drive through the twisting country roads towards the north Devon coast. The weather had deteriorated since she'd left Bath and crossing Exmoor in the dark during a December gale wasn't for the fainthearted.

It wasn't until the first snowflakes began to fall that Millie started to panic.

My car is not going to break down, she kept telling herself. I am not going to get stuck in a snow drift. That tree is not going to fall down and crush me and I am not going to meet the beast of Bodmin which might just happen to have strayed across the border from Cornwall in order to gobble me up.

Suddenly, a pony crossed the road ahead of her, its thick winter coat a bright chestnut in the headlights from the car. Millie watched as it disappeared through the stunted, windswept trees at the side of the road. Even in the height of summer, this was an eerie landscape, she reflected.

Just get to the cottage, she told herself. You're almost there.

She'd stayed at the cottage on many family holidays but she'd never driven there herself and she was unfamiliar with the roads which crossed the moor. It was also impossible to glimpse that first magical sighting of the sea at this time of day. Still, even with the snow falling, she couldn't resist winding her window down a few inches and inhaling the fresh, salt-laden air which told her that it wasn't far now.

Cove Cottage wasn't the sort of place one found without either a map or a set of foolproof directions. Off the main road and down a little lane which ran through a dark wood, only the most observant would notice the gap in the trees and the pothole-ridden track which declined steeply towards the sea. Lined with thick gorse which blazed the richest yellow whatever time of year it was, the track twisted and turned as it descended, with steep cliffs rising to the right and acres of thick bracken to the left. It was a wild, windswept place which blew away the cobwebs and entered the soul of all who visited.

Slowing down as she reached the wood, Millie looked out for the gap in the trees, turning slowly into it. The track was wet and muddy and she could see more snowflakes in the headlights. At least she was nearly there, she thought. As long as the car kept going until she reached the cottage. It was at least half a mile from the road, she remembered, and she wouldn't like to have to trudge down the track with her suitcase in the dark.

Turning the last corner, she caught her first glimpse of Cove Cottage which was strange because she shouldn't have been able to see it at all.

'The lights are on,' she said aloud, turning the car to park it on the grass beside an old outbuilding used to store wood for the stove in the living room. Perhaps Aunt Louise had asked the cleaner to leave the lights on for her.

She switched the car engine off and, for a moment, sat in the dark. If the lights hadn't been on in the cottage, it would have been pitch black. Luckily, she'd remembered to bring a torch with her and she fumbled for it now in the depths of her handbag.

As soon as she opened the car door, she heard the roar of the wind and relished the freshness of the air that whipped around her. The snow had just stopped and Millie craned her neck back and smiled as she took in the immensity of the night sky above her sewn with a thousand stars. That was one of the things she missed when living in the city. As beautiful as Bath was, the light pollution didn't allow one to admire the glorious star-spangled heavens. But the intense cold soon got the better of her and, grabbing her suitcase, she followed the thin beam of the torch towards the front door.

Fishing in her pocket for the key which she'd collected from her aunt, Millie slotted it into the lock, only it didn't turn. She tried again. And again. She was quite sure she'd got the right key because it was on the funny little key ring with the picture of an Exmoor pony on it and her aunt wouldn't have given her the wrong key, would she?

Then something occurred to Millie. There must be a key in the lock on the inside. Was the cleaner still there waiting to greet her? Millie supposed it was possible and so knocked on the door loudly so as to be heard over the wind and the roar of the sea.

But it wasn't Mrs Jemison who opened the door a moment later. It was a tall, dark-haired man.

'Can I help you?' he asked, stooping in the doorframe.

Millie stood staring at him in wide-eyed horror, her long fair hair blowing around her face. 'Who *on earth* are you?' she cried.

CHAPTER 2

'I think you'd better come in,' he said. 'We can't have you freezing to death on the doorstep.'

Millie's eyes were still wide with surprise but what else could she do but follow him into the cottage? A fire was blazing in the wood burner in the living room and Millie parked her suitcase and took off her coat and gloves.

'Can I make you a cup of tea whilst we try and work out what's going on?' the man said.

Millie nodded and watched as he moved into the open-plan kitchen. *What* was going on? She looked around the room and noticed that this strange man – whoever he was – had certainly made himself at home. There was a tumbler of whisky on a little table and a novel had been left open on the chair by the wood burner. Millie took a step towards it and saw that it was some kind of thriller. But what was this man doing here with his whisky and his thriller? Didn't he have a home of his own? Perhaps he was some kind of tramp but he'd looked too well-dressed for that with his checked shirt and Shetland wool jumper. Or perhaps he was just an opportunist who sought out empty properties at Christmas time to avoid paying the exorbitant fees which holiday homes usually cost at this time of year.

She sighed. This was the very last thing she'd expected to face after her arduous journey.

'Here you are,' he said as he left the kitchen. 'I've brought in the milk and sugar so you can make it how you like.'

She watched as he laid her aunt's flower-festooned tray on the coffee table and something inside her almost snapped at the cheek of the man to think that he could touch such things.

'Listen!' she began.

'I'm Niall,' he interrupted, as if he knew she was about to blow. 'Niall Eastwood.'

'I'm Millie Venning,' she said in return and they shook hands awkwardly.

'Louise Chambers said that I could use this cottage over Christmas,' he explained.

'Aunt Louise? You know my aunt?' Millie said, deflated.

'I'm her GP,' he said.

Millie cocked her head to one side in confusion.

'Look, there's obviously been some sort of misunderstanding. Your aunt told me the cottage was free.'

'But that's what she told *me*,' Millie said, 'otherwise I should never have driven down here.' She shook her head. 'She's getting horribly forgetful in her old age.'

'There's nothing wrong with you aunt's memory,' Niall said.

'Well, there *must* be otherwise this would never have happened.'

Niall sat down in the chair where his thriller was resting on the arm, leaving Millie standing in the middle of the room like a lost thing.

'Oh, this is ridiculous,' she said, sitting down on one of the sofas.

'Have some tea,' Niall said, making Millie frown. He sounded like a bossy parent.

Millie poured herself a cup and took a sip. He was being extremely optimistic if he thought a cup of tea was going to sort out this problem.

'How long were you planning on staying?' she asked him.

'Until New Year,' he said. 'I've got a bit of time off work and thought some sea air would do me good. Your aunt's been talking about the cottage for ages and I was delighted to take her up on her kind offer.'

Millie shifted uneasily on the sofa. 'I was planning on staying until the twenty-seventh. I'm due back at work on the twenty-eighth.'

'Where do you live?'

'In Bath. Near Sydney Gardens,' she said.

'Really? I'm just up the road in Bathwick.'

Millie nodded. She really wasn't in the mood for an exchange of pleasantries. She wanted to kick her boots off and call it a night.

'Do you always go away at Christmas?' she asked nevertheless.

'No, no,' he said. 'This is the first year.' He cleared his throat and turned to look at the fire and Millie instinctively felt that particular avenue of conversation had come to an end.

'Right,' she said, catching his eye for a brief moment and wishing that he'd picked somebody else's aunt to charm into lending him their cottage for Christmas.

'And what do you do in Bath?' he asked. 'Is your work there?'

She nodded. 'I'm a secretary at Charnwood and Hudson's – the solicitors in Queen Square.'

'Oh, right,' he said, nodding. An awkward silence fell between them and then Niall suddenly stood up. 'Look,' he said, 'this is your family's place. I'll pack my stuff and get going. It's only fair.'

Millie sighed, suddenly feeling awful at having such uncharitable thoughts. 'Don't be silly,' she said. 'It's blowing a gale out there and you'll never find any accommodation this close to Christmas. There are two bedrooms here. We'll just have to make the best of the situation until the morning.'

'It just doesn't seem right,' he continued. 'Look, we should get going, okay?'

'*We?*' Millie said.

It was then that a young dark-haired boy appeared in the living room door.

'Dad?' he said, rubbing sleepy eyes. 'What's happening?'

Millie looked at the boy and the boy looked at Millie.

'Robbie – this is Millie,' Niall explained. 'Her aunt owns the cottage.'

'Is she staying with us?' Robbie asked.

'No. We've got to go.'

'But we've only just got here,' Robbie complained.

'I know but this isn't our cottage,' Niall said.

Robbie who was, Millie guessed, about nine years old, looked confused.

'I don't want to go,' he said.

'Nobody's going anywhere,' Millie said, rising to her feet. 'Why don't we all just go to bed and talk things through in the morning? None of us could possibly think of going anywhere tonight.'

'Well, if you're sure.'

'Of course I'm sure. It's after nine, it's dark and it's snowing. It would be foolish for any of us to leave.'

Niall nodded. 'Well, let me move Robbie into my room.'

Millie shook her head. 'The sofa up against that wall pulls out into a bed,' she said. 'That'll be fine for me. I'm used to sleeping on that.'

'I won't hear of it,' Niall said. 'Tell you what, why don't you take the sofa, Robbie so Millie can have the second bedroom?'

Robbie gave a big grin, obviously thinking that the idea of sleeping on a sofa was the most exciting thing he'd ever heard of and Millie felt herself grinning back at him.

'I'll change the bedding over so you don't have to sleep on Robbie's nibbled biscuit crumbs.'

'There aren't any crumbs in my bed!' Robbie said indignantly.

Niall didn't look convinced. 'You are a secret biscuit muncher and you know it!' he said, ruffling his son's dark hair. 'Now, let's get moving so Millie can turn in for the night.'

They left the room and Millie sipped her tea whilst she listened to the sounds of movement coming from upstairs and, a few minutes later, Robbie appeared with his bedding all ready to camp out for the night on the sofa.

'I've changed the bedding upstairs,' Niall said, 'so it's all ready for you.'

'Thank you,' Millie said, watching as Niall began to assemble the sofa bed. 'Are you sure you'll be all right in here?' she added, turning to see young Robbie wrestling with his duvet.

'He'll love it, won't you, Robs?' Niall said from the door.

'Well, goodnight,' she said to Robbie as he knocked his pillow into shape.

'Night, Millie,' he said. 'Thank you for letting us stay.'

Millie smiled. There, she thought, was one well-brought up boy even if his father had told him to say that to her when they'd been upstairs.

'I'm ever so sorry about the muddle,' Niall said a moment later as the two of them went upstairs, Niall carrying Millie's suitcase like the perfect gentleman.

'It's okay,' Millie said. 'I'm sure it can be sorted out. It was just a bit of a surprise to find somebody here, that's all.'

'Of course,' he said. 'I can imagine.'

They were on the landing now and the two of them stood awkwardly for a moment.

'I'm in here,' he said, nodding to the master bedroom with the tiny en suite. 'Unless you wanted this room?'

'No, no,' she said quickly. 'I'll be fine in there,' she said, nodding to the smaller bedroom on the other side of the landing.

'I'll say goodnight, then,' he said and Millie nodded.

'Goodnight,' she said, watching as he disappeared into the master bedroom.

Millie took her suitcase into the other room. And then something occurred to her. Where was Robbie's mother? Was Niall a single father or was he divorced? Perhaps he was a no-good cheat in the same mould as her ex but surely Robbie's mother wouldn't have entrusted such an ex with her son for the entire length of the Christmas holiday if that was the case.

Millie shook her head as she began to unpack her suitcase. She couldn't be worrying about the private life of strangers when they would be leaving the next day and she'd be very unlikely to see them again.

She placed her travel clock on the bedside table. It was ten o'clock and much too early for Millie to go to bed but a nice warm bath and a leisurely read could be looked forward to.

She wondered what Niall was doing. It was odd imagining him in the room that she'd looked forward to staying in but she couldn't possibly be angry with him as it certainly wasn't his fault that he found himself in there. Poor Aunt Louise had obviously got in a muddle. A muddle that they'd be sure to sort out in the morning.

It was sometime in the middle of the night when Millie was woken up. She took a few moments to work out where she was and then a few minutes after that to work out what it was that had woken her. It was crying.

She got out of bed, switching the bedside lamp on and then finding her slippers and jumper before the cold engulfed her. Then, she tiptoed across the room and quietly opened the bedroom door. The landing light had been left on and she could hear Niall's voice coming from downstairs. Slowly descending, she heard his gentle words.

'It's all right, Robs,' he was saying. 'It was just a nightmare. It can't hurt you. It's gone now.'

'It was real, Dad,' Robbie said. 'I was really there.'

'No you weren't. It was just your imagination but it's all gone now.'

Millie bit her lip. Poor little boy, she thought, as she tiptoed back up the stairs to her bedroom.

CHAPTER 3

Millie had always been an early riser, even if it was the middle of winter and even though she was officially on holiday, and she was the first up at Cove Cottage the next morning with one task in mind.

Getting washed and dressed quickly, she sneaked downstairs so as not to wake up Robbie and, grabbing her winter coat and popping her feet into her boots, she opened the front door and walked outside. A blast of cold December wind greeted her and the roar of the sea filled her ears. She took a deep breath, fishing for her beanie hat in one of her coat pockets and flattening it onto her head. That was better, she thought. She could just about hear herself think now.

She looked around at the familiar landscape with the little brook which ran to the left of the cottage and the gorse-studded fields which had played home to many a game of hide and seek during family holidays in the past. Then, to the right, the ground sloped down towards the beach but Millie wasn't heading there. She walked a little way up the pothole-strewn track which she had bumped down the night before and then climbed up the hill, her heart pounding and instantly making her feel guilty that she was so unfit.

From the top, the landscape curved along the coastline, plummeting down to the sea in enormous dark cliffs. Today, thick grey clouds threatened to obscure the sun and there were white horses out at sea galloping towards the horizon. It was a view to revitalise even the most downtrodden of souls but Millie wasn't there for the view. She was there because it was the only place where she could get a signal for her mobile.

'Aunt Louise?' she said when her call was answered, raising her voice to be heard over the wind.

'Millie? Is that you? Are you all right, dear?'

'Yes, I'm fine.'

'Good, good.'

'But there's a man at the cottage.'

'Pardon?'

'A *man*. He says he's your doctor and he's here with his son.'

'Did you know about that? Did you say he could stay in the cottage over Christmas?'

'What, dear? You're cracking up. I'm losing you!'

'Don't you hang up on me, Aunt Louise,' Millie shouted down the phone. 'Don't you dare.' But her aunt had gone, leaving her none the wiser as to the situation she found herself in.

Millie tried her aunt's number again but service had been lost and, with a great sigh, she put her phone in her pocket and headed back down the hill towards the cottage. What was she going to tell Niall, she wondered? She felt like the Biblical keeper of the inn turning him and his little boy out just before Christmas but what choice did she have? They found themselves in a tricky situation that was not of their making.

It was just as she was approaching the front door that she heard a voice coming from the beach.

'Millie!'

She turned and saw Niall and Robbie.

'Come and join us!' Niall shouted.

She sighed. She would go for a walk with them to be sociable and *then* she'd turn them out.

'Good morning!' Niall said as she reached them, his dark hair blowing wildly around his face. He was wearing an enormous winter coat but the zip was undone, revealing a thick woollen jumper in a deep amber colour that reminded Millie of autumn bracken. 'We're just going for a quick walk along the shore. It's the best way to work up an appetite for breakfast, don't you think?'

Millie nodded.

'Robbie saw you up on the hill.'

'Yes. I was trying to get phone signal,' Millie confessed.

'Any luck?'

'Not really,' she said.

'I'm trying not to think about the outside world. My mobile is off and I didn't even bring my laptop with me.'

'Not that there's WIFI at the cottage,' Millie said to him, 'even if you did have your laptop.'

'Exactly,' he said. 'This is just the sort of place I've been looking for my whole life.'

She smiled lightly, feeling slightly guilty that his stay was going to be so short. 'I guess being a GP is pretty full-time.'

'Oh, yes!' he said with a sigh. 'It's hard to get away sometimes but you have to make yourself. I think that's why your aunt forced this place upon me. She wouldn't leave me alone until I promised her I'd take a proper break.'

'That sounds like Aunt Louise,' Millie said. 'She likes taking care of people.'

'She's a very special person,' Niall said.

'She is,' Millie said, taking a quick look at Niall and wondering what his relationship with her aunt was like. Aunt Louise clearly liked this man enough to give him the keys to Cove Cottage. If only she'd been able to talk to her more and find out a little more about him.

They headed down to the beach, clambering over the jagged black rocks that were lethally wet underfoot.

'Okay?' Niall asked, offering a gallant hand.

'I've been doing this for years,' Millie said and then slipped. 'Ooops! Pride before a fall!'

Niall grinned.

How good it felt to be back, she thought, her feet hitting the sand at last. The sandy part of the beach stretched for a good few miles but was covered in pebbles and rocks with a flat black plateaux rising up out of it. It was a landscape which looked more like that of Lanzarote than the English coast and Millie loved it. It was a place full of secret caves and deep, dark pools and, what she liked even more was the fact that only a few locals knew of its existence so one could always find a space to call one's own. Today, it was just the three of them which didn't surprise Millie on a blustery December morning. She watched as Robbie raced across the sand, leaping over pools of water and climbing over some of the smooth black rocks which lay on the beach like dinosaur eggs.

'Niall?' she began.

'Yes?' He turned to face her and she noticed his bright blue eyes for the first time. They reminded her of the summer sea. She shook her head, not wishing to be distracted by such things.

'I heard Robbie crying in the night. Is he okay?' she asked.

'I'm so sorry we woke you.'

'Don't worry,' she said. 'I was just concerned.'

'Well, that's very kind of you,' he said. 'It took me by surprise, I have to say. I thought he was getting on all right but stress can make things worse, I think, and perhaps sleeping in a strange place brought it on again.'

'Brought what on?' Millie asked.

Niall stared out to sea before answering.

'I'm afraid Christmas isn't an easy time for us,' he began. 'It was Christmas Eve two years ago when my wife died.'

'Oh, Niall!' Millie cried in shock. 'I'm so sorry.'

He nodded but didn't speak for a moment – he just stood watching the grey waves crashing onto the shore.

'What happened?' Millie asked at last.

He closed his eyes before continuing.

'She – Emma – was driving back from the supermarket. She'd already done the big Christmas shop but remembered a few of those little items that just make the holidays complete. You know the silly things like Turkish Delight and sugared almonds?'

'We always had Turkish Delight at Christmas,' she said.

'Exactly,' he said. 'Anyway, she was driving through town on the way home when a car came speeding through the red lights at a junction. Emma lost control of her car and smashed into a wall. The doctors believe she was killed instantly. There was nothing anybody could do and the people responsible didn't stop. Joy riders, police told us.'

'God! I'm so sorry,' Millie said, tears stinging her eyes at the horror of what had happened to him.

Niall nodded. 'But the worst thing about it was that Robbie was in the car with her.'

'Oh, no!'

'He was so *so* lucky to have survived,' he said.

'Was he badly hurt?'

'He broke his arm and suffered cuts and bruises but it's what he's suffering emotionally that's really worrying.'

'Of course,' Millie said. 'I can't imagine what he's gone through.'

'It hurts me so much that I can't help him.'

'Oh, but I'm sure you do – just by being there for him.'

'We thought it might be easier being away from home but I'm not sure of the effect it's having on Robbie now. Not after last night's upset. So, perhaps it's best if we leave anyway.'

Millie bit her lip as she remembered that she was about to turn them away from Cove Cottage.

'But you *have* to stay,' she suddenly said.

'Pardon?'

'You can't think of going.'

Niall turned his blue gaze on her again. 'But I thought—'

'Never mind what you thought. I really want you to say.'

'You're not just saying that out of pity, are you? Because that would be really awful.'

She shook her head. 'It's not pity. You simply *must* stay and that's an end of it.'

Niall looked confused. 'But what will you do?'

'I'll stay too,' she said with a little shrug. 'If you don't mind, that is?'

'Of course I don't mind.'

'I mean, there's room enough, isn't there?'

'Sure,' he said, 'but won't you mind knocking into me and Robbie all the time? Don't you want the place to yourself?'

She gave a little smile. 'I spend most of my time living on my own. I think it might actually be nice to have some company for a change.'

'But I can't promise what kind of company we'll be,' he said.

'I'm not asking for any promises.'

They looked steadily at each other for a moment.

'Well, if you're absolutely sure,' he said, his eyebrows raised in question.

'I *am*,' she said, giving him a little smile of encouragement.

'That's great!' he said. 'I'd really like to give Robbie a chance here. I think it could do him a lot of good. Is it all right if I tell him?'

She nodded.

'ROBS!' he called out across the beach. Robbie looked up from where he was examining a heap of slimy seaweed. 'Millie says we can stay at the cottage.'

Millie watched as the boy's face lit up and then he did something totally unexpected – he raced across the beach, leaping over the rocks and pools, and launched himself into Millie's arms.

'Thank you!' he cried. 'Thank you!'

CHAPTER 4

As they walked back to the cottage together, Millie felt the sting of tears in her eyes and she knew they had absolutely nothing to do with the cold wind. She watched as Robbie ran ahead of them, the hood of his coat bobbing up and down and she felt so sad as she thought of what that dear boy had gone through and, indeed, what he was still going through. He was far too young to be without his mother but she could see just how much Niall adored him and he was obviously trying to do his very best for his little boy.

Thinking about it now, Millie felt terrible for being angry with Aunt Louise for letting her cottage to a stranger when she had only been trying to give a grieving father and son some peace. She wondered if her aunt had ever met Niall's wife or, indeed, his son, or did she only know Niall on a professional level? And did it really matter? All that mattered was that her aunt had tried to do a kindness and it was up to Millie to make sure that he had just the sort of holiday that her aunt had had in mind for him and his boy.

Climbing up from the beach, she watched as Niall walked towards his four-wheel-drive which she hadn't spotted the night before, and it was then that she noticed there was a Christmas tree in the back of it.

'You brought a tree with you?' she asked.

'Of course,' he said. 'It wouldn't be Christmas without a tree, would it?'

'I suppose not.'

'We arrived after dark so we didn't have a chance to unpack it.'

'You travelled with it from Bath?'

'Yep!' he said. 'The car smelt wonderful but it did keep tickling Robbie's ears.'

'Yes!' Robbie said. 'It did.'

Millie smiled. 'Would you like a hand with it?'

'I should be okay but you can grab the bucket if you like and make sure the doors are open.'

Millie picked up the bucket and unlocked the front door and then helped to guide Niall with the tree. It wasn't the biggest tree in the world but, once it was placed in the living room, it seemed to fill it.

'Wow!' Robbie said.

'Wow!' Millie echoed.

'Ow!' Niall said as he popped the tree into its bucket. 'Got poked in the nose.'

Robbie laughed. 'I got poked in the ear for over three hours!'

'You did indeed,' Niall said. 'Anyway, there's plenty of time to decorate it but that can't possibly be attempted on an empty stomach. Who's up for some drop scones?'

'ME!' Robbie yelled.

'Millie?' Niall asked.

'Oh? Yes, thank you.'

'Good,' he said, getting to work in the kitchen which adjoined the living room.

'Dad makes the *best* drops scones in the whole world,' Robbie enthused.

Millie smiled and watched as Niall moved around the kitchen with the sort of ease that she never had. It was rather nice having breakfast made for you, she thought, and something that she'd never experienced before. James certainly hadn't been one to make breakfast for her whenever she'd stayed with him. He'd been far more likely to tell her the bread was stale and warn her that it might actually be mouldy which it very often was. But she had to admit that Niall with a whisk in his hand was rather a pleasant sight and the result was pretty good too.

'These are excellent!' Millie said as, sitting next to Robbie at the breakfast bar, she took her first mouthful. 'And Devon flower honey too – my favourite.'

Niall smiled. 'Mine too,' he said.

'I prefer golden syrup,' Robbie said, 'or chocolate spread. Or marshmallow fluff. Or all three at once!'

Niall shook his head in despair. 'Honey is better for you,' he told his son.

'Dad's a really good cook,' Robbie told Millie, 'but he doesn't get much time to do it.'

'That's right,' Niall said. 'Does it seem odd to want to spend more time in the kitchen?'

'Not at all,' Millie said. 'Not if it's what you love doing.'

'Maybe I'll try out some recipes on you,' he said.

'Sounds good to me,' Millie said. 'I'm afraid I don't cook at all. My idea of breakfast is something out of a box. Lunch is usually a bought sandwich and dinner is something that is flung into a microwave.'

Niall frowned. 'That all sounds rather–' he paused.

'Sad?'

He shook his head. 'I wasn't going to say that.'

'But you were thinking it?' Millie said. 'It's just that I always seem to be in a rush and I'm so tired when I get home and it's just me and it doesn't really seem worth thinking about a recipe with thirty different ingredients that will need washing or peeling or preparing for a meal that only lasts ten minutes.'

Millie was aware that both Niall and Robbie were staring at her.

'But food isn't just about filling a gap or nutrition,' Niall said. 'It's the stuff of life and there are so many wonderful flavours and different ways to prepare something that could be fun too.'

'Dad sometimes lets me make things,' Robbie said.

'What do you like to make?' Millie asked.

'A mess usually,' Niall said.

Robbie pulled face at his dad. 'I like making cakes,' he said with great authority.

'I like eating cakes,' Millie said.

'Well, that sounds like a plan,' Niall said, and the three of them laughed.

Millie did the washing up after they'd all finished and made herself and Niall a cup of tea which they drank by the wood burner whilst Robbie amused himself with a Lego set.

'How often does your aunt get down here?' he asked Millie.

'I can't remember the last time she came,' Millie said. 'I've offered to bring her but she doesn't like being away from home these days.'

Niall nodded. 'That's understandable,' he said.

Millie looked across at him and realised that he would probably know a lot more about her aunt's health than she did but, of course, he wouldn't be permitted to talk about it.

'Her confidence has taken a real knock since the arthritis set in,' Millie said, 'and she's in a lot of pain. I think she likes the comfort of her own home and being surrounded by people who are able to keep an eye on her.'

Niall nodded again. 'So, the cottage is empty most of time?'

'Oh, no. It's let out during the holidays and it's usually very popular. I can't think why it wasn't booked this week.'

'I'm not surprised it's popular. It's the most beautiful location I've ever seen.'

'Yes,' Millie said. 'It takes some beating, doesn't it? Of course, growing up with this as our holiday retreat, I was totally spoilt. Only you don't realise that when you're a kid, do you? I remember my desperation to take holidays abroad as soon as I was able to and my intense disappointment to find that the coasts of Spain and Italy and France aren't really any better. They might be a tad warmer but I've never really minded the English weather. It's all part and parcel with our countryside, isn't it? I mean, without the rain, it wouldn't be so green and lush, would it?'

He grinned.

'What?' Millie asked.

'That's a very positive way of looking at bad weather,' he said.

'If you don't like the English weather, you really shouldn't be holidaying in December.'

'That is true enough,' he conceded. 'You know, we always used to favour holidays abroad. When I first met Emma, we'd be jetting off to Sri Lanka or India or going on safari in some hot dusty part of Africa.'

'And did you like it?'

'I liked it well enough,' he said, 'but I'm really beginning to think that a pretty corner of the English countryside suits me very well these days. Does that make me sound horribly old?'

Millie smiled. 'Not at all.' She looked at his face and wondered if it would be rude to ask just how old he was. He didn't look that much older than her. His hair was thick and dark but there were light lines around his eyes when he smiled which would place him in his mid-forties at least. It was a nice face, she thought – the kind of face that wouldn't frighten patients when they entered his room at the surgery. It was a face that would help patients open up to him, she thought. A kind, compassionate and handsome face.

Handsome? Where had *that* word come from, she wondered? Suddenly, she was up on her feet. She cleared her throat.

'I'm erm–'

'Going out? We were actually going to head into Tarlsford for some supplies today and you're welcome to join us if you like. It might be the last chance for a while.'

'What – is snow forecast?' Millie asked. 'We're not going to get snowed in, are we?'

'I meant that it's Christmas Eve,' he said.

'So it is,' Millie said. 'I'd forgotten.'

'How could you forget that?' Robbie demanded as he entered the room with his coat already on.

She grinned. 'I have absolutely no idea,' she said.

The pretty market town of Tarlsford was the sort of place that holidaymakers who were lucky enough to discover it would return to time and time again. Set in a picturesque valley amongst the Devon hills, it boasted a bakery, a florist's, a grocery store, two pubs and a post office. There was even a tiny secondhand bookshop where all were welcome even if you were soaked to the skin after walking across Exmoor or sporting a pair of muddy boots.

'Tourist shopping first?' Niall suggested and Millie nodded. There then followed a very pleasant hour of poking around the bookshop. Millie had always adored secondhand books. She adored new ones too but there was something rather special about owning a pre-loved novel especially if it came with a few dog-eared pages or pencil notes in the margins. Her little flat in Bath had books in every room from the latest bestselling novel to hardback volumes of poetry from the early part of the last century with silk-like pages which felt so smooth to the touch. Today, she found a pretty edition of a Thomas Hardy novel. Niall found a curious book on herbal medicines from Tudor England and Robbie found a basket of old comics and had chosen three rather tatty ones.

'Are you *sure* you want those?' Niall asked him.

'Yeah!' Robbie said. 'Why?'

'Because they look as though they've been devoured by a mad dog.'

Robbie shook his head and took them to the counter where an old man in a big overcoat and a pair of orange fingerless gloves popped them in a brown paper bag for him.

'Here,' Niall said to Millie, taking her book from her. Allow me.'

'Oh, there's no need.'

'It's just a tiny way of saying thank you for letting us stay,' he said.

'You don't need to say thank you.'

'But I shall anyway,' he told her with great authority.

As they left the shop with their bags of books and comics, Millie thought about ringing her aunt because she was sure to be able to get a signal in town but what would be the point? She'd been going to cross question Aunt Louise to find out what was going on but, watching Niall and Robbie filling a basket in the local grocery store a few minutes later, she realised how lucky she was to be spending Christmas with them.

Millie nipped out of the shop to call her aunt to let her know everything was okay at the cottage but there was no answer. After leaving a message, she realised that she had a few messages of her own and she was just listening to them when Niall and Robbie came out of the shop. The messages were all from James. He was sorry. He'd made a mistake and he wanted her back.

Don't let a few silly affairs come between us! he had the nerve to say. They meant nothing to me!

Well, he'd made Millie feel as if *she* meant nothing to *him* and so she deleted all seven of his messages one after the other.

'Everything okay?' Niall asked as Millie returned her phone to her bag.

'Everything's fine,' she said but she couldn't help feeling a great weight of sadness in her heart at that moment. She'd thought that coming to Devon would help her put James out of her mind – that he couldn't follow her to her special place – but he was still able to reach out and upset her no matter how many miles of wild countryside lay between them.

'Let's get back, shall we?' she said, looking forward to returning to the coast where the bad mobile phone reception would help to block James's calls.

It was one of those magical days where sunshine and frost played happily together and the moors looked beautiful. The tawny-coloured bracken had been turned silver and great puddles and little streams had frozen over.

'It's getting pretty cold now,' Niall said.

'Cold enough for snow?' Robbie asked.

'You know, it just might be,' Niall said. 'I've not listened to the forecast but we might be in for a white Christmas. You never know.'

Millie smiled from her place on the backseat. A white Christmas, she thought. She couldn't remember the last time she'd experienced that.

Niall's Range Rover bumped down the track to Cove Cottage and

Millie couldn't help thinking how much more suited it was to the terrain than her own little car. As they came round the final bend, she sighed with pleasure as she saw the great waves of the sea.

'I never tire of that view,' she said.

'I'm kind of getting used to it myself,' Niall said.

'Me too,' Robbie agreed and they pulled up alongside the wood store.

'At least we've got enough logs to see us through if the worst comes to the worst,' Niall said.

'You mean if we're snowed in until spring?' Millie said.

'*Cool!*' Robbie said.

Niall laughed and watched as Robbie leapt out of the car and tore across the grass towards the brook.

'Don't be too long!' he called after him and then his attention turned to Millie. 'Are you all right?' he asked as he grabbed the shopping bags out of the car.

'Yes, why?' Millie asked, conscious of his gaze upon her.

'You were a bit quiet on the way back,' he said. 'You–' he paused, 'looked thoughtful.'

'Did I?' she said.

'It's part of my job to read faces, he said. 'I'm sorry if I pried. I didn't mean to.'

'No, no,' she said quickly. 'It's just – well – there's a bit to be thoughtful about at the moment.'

He held her gaze for a moment longer. 'I'm a pretty good listener,' he said. 'If you ever want to talk.'

'Thanks,' she said, 'but it's nothing. Nothing that time and space can't cure anyway.'

CHAPTER 5

It was good to be back at the cottage. Niall soon had the wood burner lit and roaring, and Millie and Robbie put the shopping away. She watched as the young boy then settled down on the floor by the fire with his nose deep inside one of his comics. Millie smiled as she remembered doing just the same thing when she'd been his age only it had been novels about ponies rather than comics about superheroes which had obsessed her.

Leaving the room, she climbed the stairs to her bedroom to find her slippers. She felt at ease enough with Niall and Robbie to wear her furry pink and white slippers. But, as she was slipping her feet into their warm depths, something strange and quite unexpected happened. Millie found she was crying and not just a few casual tears either but great chest-racking sobs. What on earth was happening? Where had all these tears come from? But she knew where. It had been listening to James's voice on her phone. Message after message. It had stirred up all the old memories again. Memories she'd hoped had been fading and which she'd been bottling up on the drive back to the cottage.

She wasn't sure how long she had been crying for but, when she heard the knock on her bedroom door, she realised that she must have been making quite a noise.

'Millie?'

She cursed herself silently and quickly pulled a tissue from her pocket but it didn't stand a chance of mopping up her tears quickly enough.

'Are you okay?' Niall said, entering the room even though she hadn't invited him to do so.

'I'm fine,' she said, not daring to look up at him.

'Well, you don't look or sound fine. Here – come and sit down.' He guided her towards the bed and they sat down next to each other without speaking. Millie mopped her eyes with her tissue and took a deep breath.

'I – erm –,' she stopped and blew her nose. 'I recently broke up with my boyfriend,' she said and then gave a strange sort of laugh.

'*Boyfriend!* That's *such* a ridiculous word for a woman in her thirties to use, isn't it? But he wasn't ever going to be anything more as it turns out. We'd been together for about six years and I really thought we were going to go the distance.'

'I'm sorry,' Niall said.

She shook her head. 'It's silly to get upset about it.'

'No it isn't,' he said. 'You've obviously invested a lot of time and energy and love into this relationship.'

'But it's nothing compared to what you've been through,' she said.

'It's different – that's all,' he told her.

'I thought I'd done all my crying,' she said. 'I'm so mad at myself.'

'Don't be mad,' he said. 'It's a perfectly normal way of coping with things. "Better out than in" – that's what we doctors are meant to say, isn't it?'

Millie couldn't help smiling at that. 'So, have you got a quick cure for me, doctor?' she asked.

'I wish I had,' he said, 'but broken hearts take their time to heal, I'm afraid.'

She took a deep breath and then sighed it out. 'I don't think it's *completely* broken,' she said. 'But it is very bruised.'

He nodded. 'That's only to be expected.'

They sat quietly together on the bed, the sound of a robin's song outside the window. It felt strangely intimate and Millie suddenly remembered that, although they were sharing the cottage and she'd just told him something very personal, this man was still essentially a stranger to her but, before she could do or say anything, he had leapt up from the bed.

'Listen,' he said gently, 'come downstairs and help us with the tree. We're going to decorate it and it would probably be a good idea to have a woman's eye.' He cocked his head to one side in a pleading manner that completely won her over.

'I'd be delighted to help,' she said, mopping her eyes again and giving her nose a thoroughly good blow after Niall had left the room.

When Millie entered the living room, Robbie was on the floor surrounded by tinsel and boxes of baubles which shone like jewels from a fairytale.

'Come on, Dad!' he said. 'Get the lights on.'

'Yes, sir!' Niall said as he picked up the box which contained a long rope of golden fairy lights. Millie and Robbie watched as Niall threaded them expertly through the tree.

'You've done that before,' Millie said.

'Oh, yes,' he said, switching them on a moment later so that the deep gold sparkled in the green depths of the tree.

'Now tinsel!' Robbie said, leaping to his feet with the long snakes of silver and gold.

'Give Millie some,' Niall said and Robbie handed a length of silver tinsel to her.

It didn't take long before the tree was garlanded in silver and golden splendour.

'Baubles now!' Robbie declared.

'Each of us chooses a colour for the tree, don't we?' Niall said. 'Emma chose gold. There might be fifty million colours in the world and she'd always choose gold, wouldn't she, Robbie?'

Robbie nodded silently and Millie felt her heart ache for him.

'Of course there was that year you cheated,' Niall said to his son, moving forward to ruffle his dark hair.

'I didn't cheat!' Robbie said.

Niall grinned. 'Robbie found the most outrageous stripy baubles. How many coloured stripes on each one?'

'About eighty,' Robbie said.

Niall and Millie laughed.

'What colour have you chosen this year, Robbie?' she asked.

'Blue,' he said.

'And I've chosen silver,' Niall said.

'Silver, blue and gold,' Millie said. 'Sounds lovely and very wintery. It's a brilliant idea to choose a colour each.'

'What colour would you choose, Millie?' Robbie asked.

'Oh!' Millie said, caught off-guard. 'Probably something girly like pink.'

Robbie wrinkled his nose in disgust.

'Or purple,' she added quickly.

'Purple's better,' he said and Millie smiled. 'Is that what you've got on your tree?'

'I don't have a tree,' she said.

'You don't have a tree?' Robbie said in astonishment.

'Nope!' she said. 'There doesn't really seem much point when it's just me who'll see it.'

'What decorations do you have, then?' Robbie asked.

'I don't really do Christmas,' she said.

'You don't *do* Christmas?' Niall asked, looking perplexed.

Millie blushed. 'Well, it's just me on my own most years, you see. It doesn't really seem worth all the effort other than putting up a few Christmas cards.'

Robbie looked at his dad as if to ask if this was normal adult behaviour but Niall looked as nonplussed as his son.

'Really,' Millie said, 'it's so much fuss and bother.'

The expression on Robbie's face told Millie he'd have been less shocked if she'd sworn really badly so she thought she'd better shut up.

Silently and carefully, the three of them worked their way around the tree with the coloured baubles placing a gold one here, a silver one there and a dazzling blue one in between. Then came the other decorations which were kept in a round sweetie tin. There were gold stars, little wooden reindeer, cheery red Santas and delicate silver angels.

'Put the main lights out, Dad,' Robbie said after every decoration had been placed on the tree and Niall got up to turn the main lights off and everyone gasped when they looked at the tree. It glittered, glistened and glowed and all three of them sighed and wowed in delight.

'That's the loveliest tree I've ever seen,' Millie said.

'It's not bad, is it?' Niall said.

'It's *fantastic!*' Robbie said.

The three of them stood in silent wonder, watching the golden lights twinkling gently amongst the foliage and decorations. It was a magical moment that Millie couldn't remember experiencing since childhood. James had never been that bothered about Christmas and had either spent it with his family in Scotland or had persuaded Millie to go away with him – always somewhere warm and sunny like the Canary islands or Morocco – which had been very nice at the time but Millie realised now that she had forgotten the joys of a truly English Christmas with the crisp bright frosts outside and a roaring stove inside.

'I promise I'll never have another Christmas without a tree,' she said and Robbie grinned at her.

'More logs,' Niall suddenly said. 'Then lunch.'

'Let me,' she said. 'Even I know how to make cheesy pasta.'

'Yum!' Robbie said as he collapsed onto the floor again with one of his comics.

As Millie was preparing lunch, it crossed her mind that she was in the middle of nowhere with a stranger in possession of an axe but Niall had proved himself as much as a man could in two short days. He was kind, caring and, as far as she could tell, perfectly sane. Indeed, the compassion he'd shown her when he'd caught her crying had touched her deeply. She paused for a moment, a block of cheddar in one hand and a grater in the other. Niall Eastwood was a lovely man. A lovely man who also happened to be very handsome.

Handsome.

There was that word again – the word that was liable to get a girl into trouble because the last handsome man she'd been involved with had broken – well, *bruised* – her heart. There was no doubt in her mind that Niall was a handsome man with his brilliant blue eyes and thick dark hair but it was more than that. She loved watching him with Robbie. He was so kind and patient with his son and there was such an easy affection between the two of them that she'd never had with either of her parents. It was lovely to watch.

Just then, he walked back into the living room, his arms full of chopped logs. Millie felt herself blushing as she stared at him. He looked so strong and earthy. She shook her head, embarrassed by her thoughts.

'You okay?' he said as he looked across at her. 'You look very red. Perhaps I'd better not put any more on the fire just yet. Not if it's warm enough already.'

'Yes,' Millie said, quickly busying herself with the cheese. 'It's quite warm enough, isn't it?'

After lunch, there was a certain amount of lounging around on the sofas before Robbie came up with the suggestion of going out.

Millie looked out of the tiny cottage window. The view beyond the faded chintz curtains wasn't a tempting one. The sky had darkened since lunchtime and the wind had whipped itself up into a frenzy but the short days meant that one had to grab every opportunity of fresh air and they would have the whole of the evening to sprawl in front of the wood burner. So the three of them got up, shoved their feet into extra thick woolly socks and boots and quickly doubled their body sizes with the number of jumpers and coats and scarves they put on in order to protect themselves against the bitter cold. The north Devon coast could be a pretty unforgiving place weather wise at the best of times but, in the depths of winter, it could be positively brutal.

Leaving the cosy warmth of the cottage, they headed straight down to the beach, following Robbie as he led the way with great determination, his hooded head bowed down as he pushed himself through the wind.

They had the beach to themselves once again which wasn't really surprising on a cold Christmas Eve. Most sensible people would be tucked up in their homes for the duration of the holiday. Millie watched as Robbie grabbed a long piece of driftwood and made three enormous circles in the wet sand before stomping in the middle of each one.

'I wish we could get away together more often,' Niall said, 'but work is always so crazy.'

Millie looked at him. 'When was your last holiday?' she asked him.

'The summer before Emma died,' he said. 'We did a fly drive to the States. Saw all the famous places like Disneyland and Los Angeles and took a boat trip out to Alcatraz in San Francisco and then flew to New York and hit Broadway. Emma used to love musical theatre.'

'Sounds like an amazing holiday.'

'A once in a lifetime one,' he said. 'Only it seems a lifetime ago now. Another me, you know?'

Millie nodded. 'You okay?' she asked as he gazed out into the grey depths of the wild winter sea, the dark clouds scudding fast and low across the horizon.

'It was about this time of day two years ago that the accident happened.'

Millie swallowed hard, not knowing how to respond to such a declaration. But she instinctively knew that it would be worse to say nothing than to say something clichéd.

'I'm so sorry, Niall,' she said and, before she realised what she was doing, she'd reached out towards him and had placed one of her gloved hands on his. He turned to look at her and she felt herself blushing. 'What was she like?' she dared to ask him.

'Emma?' he said her name slowly, as if lingering on it might bring her back. 'She was warm and funny. She loved to laugh. She was always teasing me and playing practical jokes on me because I'm so serious.'

'Are you?'

He nodded. 'I can be,' he said. 'I need loosening up every so often and Emma could always be relied upon to do that for me.'

'Did she have a job?' Millie asked.

'She worked part time in a little shop in town. One of those places that women seem to love that sells nothing but crockery and cushions.'

'Oh yes. I *adore* those kinds of shops!' Millie said.

'She was forever filling our home with teacups and candles. You can't move in our house without knocking over something printed with flowers. It's still so hard to look at all those bits and pieces because I know she chose them and handled them and placed them in our home with such care. I'm terrified of them sometimes. Robbie broke a little jug just a few days after she died and he wouldn't stop crying for hours.'

'But those *things* aren't Emma,' Millie said gently. 'You mustn't be so worried about them. She loved them – yes. But she loved you and Robbie more. Much more.'

'What a sweetheart you are,' he said and, once again, Millie felt her face flushing with colour. 'Come on. Robbie's leaving us behind.'

She watched as he walked along the shoreline, his thick boots dipping into the water and she followed in his footsteps, the waves playing a dangerous game with the low cut of her wellies. Robbie was a little dot in the distance, his arms windmilling around his body as he moved across the sand in a crazy dance. As she watched him, she realised that she was becoming very attached to this broken family and she couldn't help wondering if it was fate that had brought her to the cottage at the same time as Niall and Robbie.

CHAPTER 6

When Millie opened her eyes on Christmas morning, the light in the bedroom felt different and, immediately, she knew what it was.

'Snow!'

She leapt out of bed with the excitement of a child and ran towards the window, drawing back the curtains and blinking hard at the bright white that greeted her. Snow on Christmas morning. How many times did that happen? It had certainly never happened at Cove Cottage – not as far as she could remember.

She looked out across the sloping bank, her gaze journeying along the gentle snow-covered curves of the fields. The bracken and the gorse were now strange mountainous shapes and the sky looked as if it was still heavy with snow yet to fall.

Getting washed and dressed, Millie went downstairs to see if Niall and Robbie were up.

'Morning!' she called as she entered the living room, gasping as she saw its transformation. For a moment, she stood in the door, almost afraid to enter. This was no longer her domain – it belonged to Niall and his son and she wasn't sure she had a place there.

'Millie!' Robbie cried, looking up from where he was sitting on the carpet, a huge squashy present in his hands.

'Come in, come in!' Niall said.

'I don't want to intrude,' she said.

'Don't be silly,' Niall said.

'Don't be silly,' Robbie echoed and Millie couldn't help smiling.

'Robbie and I have been putting up the rest of the decorations we brought with us,' Niall said when he saw the look of surprise on Millie's face.

'So I see!' she said, eyeing up the berry wreath above the fireplace and the garlands of tinsel draping over the picture frames on the walls.

'Merry Christmas, Millie,' Niall said.

'Merry Christmas!' she said.

'Can you believe it snowed?' Robbie said.

'Isn't it wonderful?' Millie said.

'Robbie's been bursting to go outside but I insisted on breakfast and presents first.'

It was then that Millie noticed that music was playing.

'Is that the Nutcracker Suite?' she asked.

'It was Emma's favourite,' Niall explained. 'She listened to it every Christmas. Some people like Bing Crosby or something cheesy from the seventies but she loved Tchaikovsky, didn't she, Robbie?'

Robbie nodded as he continued to prod his unwrapped present. Now, Millie felt even more awkward about being there. Emma was still very much a presence but it would seem that Millie was also welcome.

For ten minutes, Millie watched as Robbie tore his way through a mountain of presents. There were games she didn't recognise, a remote-controlled car, the ubiquitous itchy jumper from an auntie and countless other bits and bobs needing batteries.

'There's one for you under there,' Niall told Millie as she began to help Robbie tidy up.

'Is there?'

Niall reached under the arms of the Christmas tree and presented her with a rectangular shaped box wrapped in bright silver paper.

'Oh!' she said. 'When did you get this?'

'When your back was turned in town yesterday.'

'But I feel awful now,' she said. 'I'm afraid I didn't get you anything.'

'Are you kidding?' Niall said. 'You let us stay here.'

She smiled at him and shook her head as she tore open the silver paper to reveal a box of locally made chocolates.

'I hope you like them. I have yet to meet a woman who doesn't like chocolate,' he said.

'And never trust one that doesn't,' Millie said. 'Thank you so much.'

'If you don't like them, Millie, I'll eat them for you,' Robbie said.

'You keep away from those chocolates, Robs! You chose that fudge, remember? And I've got my Turkish Delight so we're all kitted out for some teeth-rotting fun.'

'Don't forget this present, Dad,' Robbie said, handing his father a heavy rectangular gift.

'It's from your Aunt Louise, Millie,' Niall told her. 'She really shouldn't have.'

'But she always does,' Robbie said and Millie smiled because she was well aware of her auntie's generosity.

She watched in great anticipation as Niall first held the gift in his hand.

'It's a book!' Robbie said in a bored voice.

'Don't spoil things, Robbie!'

'But it's *sooooo* obvious!' he said.

'Oh!' Millie cried a moment later when Niall had ripped open the gold paper to reveal a hardback book. He turned it around to take a good look.

'Tarka the Otter,' he said.

'Yes,' Millie said. 'It's my favourite book!'

'Is it?'

'And she's found you the original Tunnicliffe edition too.'

'The what?'

'The illustrator – take a look at the illustrations – they're exquisite,' Millie told him.

Niall flipped through the pages. 'This is rather special, isn't it?' he said.

'Oh, yes,' Millie said. 'And all set in Devon too.'

'I look forward to reading it,' he said.

'Haven't you got any presents, Millie?' Robbie asked from his home on the floor.

It was then that Millie remembered the gift that she had packed in her suitcase from her aunt and went upstairs to retrieve it. It was wrapped in the same gold paper that Niall's present had been wrapped in.

'That's not a book,' Robbie said. 'It looks too light.'

'Robs!' Niall warned him. 'Don't spoil things for Millie.'

'Just saying,' Robbie said with a huff.

Millie really had no idea what it was and was surprised on opening it to find that it was in fact, a DVD box set.

'*Dr Darby*,' she said, reading the title. ' "The misadventures of a country GP." '

'Really? That's my favourite TV show,' Niall said.

'It is?' Millie said, looking confused.

'Yes. In fact, your aunt calls *me* Dr Darby. Not very original since the show's doing so well. I'm sure no end of GPs have been given the nickname Dr Darby. Have you never seen it?'

'No,' Millie said.

'What, *never?*' Robbie said. 'We love it! We watch all the time don't we, Dad?'

Millie frowned. It seemed like a rather strange present. 'Do you think Aunt Louise has given us the wrong presents by mistake?' she asked.

'I don't know,' Niall said, opening the book again. 'Oh, I don't think she has.' He turned the book towards Millie and she saw her aunt's neat handwriting on the inside page.

To Niall with love from Louise.

'Oh,' Millie said. It was undisputedly a gift meant for Niall.

'So,' Niall said, 'your aunt has bought me your favourite book and she has bought you my favourite TV show.'

Millie nodded. 'That would certainly appear to be the case,' she said.

'Any thoughts?' Niall asked and Millie couldn't help but blush.

'Well, I–' she stopped. What was she meant to say? That her aunt was deliberately trying to match-make them? Did that mean that she had told them both they could use the cottage over Christmas, knowing that they would be thrown together? Aunt Louise had tried to match-make Millie in the past with disastrous results and Millie had been forced to put her foot down. She'd thought that her aunt had got the message so what was going on? If the mobile reception was any better at the cove then Millie was quite determined that she would get to the bottom of it.

Niall suddenly laughed.

'What is it?' Millie asked in panic.

He shook his head. 'Your aunt isn't the first woman to try to–'

'Don't say it,' Millie interrupted. 'Please don't say that word.'

'Match-make me,' Niall finished and Millie winced.

'I don't know what to say,' Millie said, feeling her face flush with shame again.

'There's nothing *to* say,' Niall said. 'It's not your fault and it's not mine.'

'But it doesn't stop me wanting to apologise,' she said. 'I'm so sorry. I had no idea. You do believe me, don't you?'

'Of course I believe you,' he said.

'Oh, God!' Millie groaned. 'Perhaps I should just go.'

'No, don't!' Niall said. 'Why should this spoil things?'

'Because I feel awkward and embarrassed,' she said honestly.

'But there's no need,' he told her. 'Really there isn't. Let's just forget about it or, at least, realise that we share a mutual friend who is under the impression that we would get on which we do, don't we?' He held her gaze for a moment and Millie could do nothing but smile at his sweetness.

'Yes,' she said at last. 'Of course we do.'

'Good,' he said. 'Let's go for a walk after breakfast.'

Millie was glad to get outside into the fresh air after the stiflingly claustrophobic atmosphere of the cottage and, stepping out into the white world, she knew that she didn't want to leave Cove Cottage even if she had to endure a couple of slightly awkward days with her aunt's 'Dr Darby'.

'Look – the sand's frozen!' Niall said as they stepped onto the beach. It crunched and crackled beneath their feet and Millie peered down at it.

'I've never seen ice on a beach before. It must be really cold,' Millie said.

Niall nodded. 'The Gulf Stream around this coast usually keeps everything fairly mild.'

They walked down to the edge of the sea and saw the swirls of ice before them. Robbie crouched down and picked up a small sheet of it.

'Wow!' he said. He couldn't have looked more impressed if it had been made of diamonds.

'It's so beautiful here even in the bleakest, coldest weather,' Millie said. 'We've had some pretty amazing family holidays here.'

'It must be glorious in the summer,' Niall said.

'Oh, it is,' Millie said. 'The perfect location for a bucket and spade holiday.'

'You have a big family?' he asked as they walked the length of the beach together, Robbie cracking as much ice as he could underfoot.

'Two brothers – Marcus and Jake. I was the youngest and forever trying to keep up with them. I guess I was quite the tomboy, clambering over rocks and climbing trees.'

Niall grinned. 'Well, there are plenty of rocks around here,' he said.

'I used to love those great flat black ones.' They watched as

Robbie looked across the beach and took off like a rocket towards the rocks.

'Careful, Robs!' Niall shouted after him but there was no stopping him.

Millie ran right after him. She had forgotten how exhilarating it was to do something as simple as run across a beach with the cold wind in your face.

'Wait for me, Robbie,' she cried but the boy wasn't going to slow down for her. There was only one thing for it – she would have to run even faster. And that's when it happened. The large black rocks were slippery even in the summer months but, today, they were lethal and Millie's left foot slipped and twisted, causing her to lose her balance and come crashing down.

'MILLIE!' Niall cried as he tore across the beach to reach her. 'Don't move!'

'I don't think I can,' Millie said, wincing in pain as both Niall and Robbie reached her.

'Are you all right?' Robbie asked.

'What *was* I thinking?' Millie said.

'Is it my fault?' Robbie said.

'No, no,' Millie assured him. 'It was me being foolish and thinking I was much younger than I am.'

'Let's see what the damage is,' Niall said.

'It's my left ankle,' she told him.

'Anything else hurt?'

'I don't think so,' Millie told him.

'Let's get you back to the cottage,' he said. 'Put your arms around my neck.'

Millie did as she was told and was soon hoisted up into Niall's arms.

'I feel such an idiot,' she complained.

'I slipped too,' Robbie said, 'but I can still walk.'

'I'm afraid my bones are a lot older than yours, Robbie,' Millie told him, realising how stupid she had been to run across the rocks like that. It was a very humbling way to learn her lesson: she most definitely wasn't a young girl any more. Mind you, held in the warm strength of Niall's arms, she wasn't sure that a young girl would have fully appreciated such a situation.

'You okay?' he asked her as they left the beach, negotiating the rocks carefully before crossing the grass towards the cottage.

'Just dying of embarrassment,' she said.

'Nobody ever died of that before,' he told her.

'There's a first time for everything,' she said, feeling truly mortified.

CHAPTER 7

Niall handed Robbie the key and he opened the door and Millie was soon stretched out on the sofa nearest the wood burner in the living room, her boots carefully removed.

'Now, let's have a look,' Niall said, removing her woolly sock and placing his hands around her bare foot.

'It's a good job there's a doctor in the house,' Millie said with a faint smile. 'I'll have to call you Dr Darby.'

'Everybody else does,' he said, grinning down at her as he carefully examined her left foot. 'How does that feel?'

'Okay – ouch!'

He nodded. 'It's just a sprain.'

'Is it?'

'Nothing to worry about with a bit of careful attention. Robbie? What do we remember with sprains?'

'RICE,' Robbie cried.

'So, we have two doctors in the house,' Millie said.

Niall laughed as Robbie ran into the kitchen.

'So, what's RICE? The diet you're putting me on?'

'No, no,' Niall said. 'It stands for Rest, Ice, Compression and Elevation.'

'So what's Robbie doing?'

'He's gone to get some ice or something else frozen that will do you good.'

'Really?' Millie said. 'Won't that be awfully COLD!' she screamed as Robbie arrived with a bag of frozen peas and placed it over her ankle.

'It's the very best thing for it,' Niall assured her. 'It will keep the swelling down.'

'It feels absolutely horrid!' she said as she watched Robbie place a cushion underneath her foot. 'Oh, I feel so stupid! Why oh *why* did I have to try and scramble over those rocks? I'm such a fool – I'm not a kid anymore.'

'I think we're all kids inside, don't you?' Niall said.

'Inside, maybe – but the rest of us ages at an alarming rate,' Millie said.

'It wasn't age that got you into trouble – it was those vicious rocks,' he pointed out.

She smiled at him. It was very kind of him to say that.

'Now,' he said, 'how about we make a start on Christmas dinner?'

From her position on the sofa, Millie could watch Niall and Robbie buzzing around the kitchen as they prepared everything for the perfect Christmas dinner.

'I feel so useless stuck on the sofa not able to do anything.'

'There's nothing for you *to* do,' Niall told her. 'Everything is under control!'

Millie smiled. She had never met a man as calm and as in control as he was. Nothing seemed to fluster him which was probably just as well given his choice of career.

For the next couple of hours, she watched father and son as they bustled around the kitchen together, peeling and chopping and basting and boiling. They even remembered – mercifully – to remove the bag of frozen peas from her ankle.

Finally, Christmas dinner with all the trimmings, including some rather fine Yorkshire puddings, was ready.

Niall had found a tray which he placed on top of a cushion so Millie didn't have to move from her new home on the sofa.

'Do I really have to eat like this?'

'You do,' Niall said. 'The longer we can keep your ankle elevated, the better.'

She sighed, knowing when she was defeated.

'Don't worry – we're eating in here with you,' Robbie announced.

'Don't you want to eat in the dining room?' Millie asked.

'We'll be fine at the breakfast bar,' Niall said, motioning to the kitchen where Robbie was busy laying things out.

'Well, it all looks amazing,' Millie said, trying to get comfortable to enjoy the feast before her. She felt completely spoilt but was glad that she had contributed with some of the food bought in town the day before and was glad she wasn't facing a lonely lunch for one from the meagre provisions she'd brought with her from her flat.

'I have to say,' Niall said, 'this is a very interesting way to eat Christmas dinner.'

Robbie giggled. 'Can we have a breakfast bar at home?' he asked.

'I don't see why not,' Niall said.

'Excellent!'

Millie smiled. 'I can't say that I'd like to repeat my Christmas meal like this again.'

'Are you okay over there?' Niall asked.

'Oh, yes,' she said quickly, not wishing to complain after all the hard work that had gone into the meal, 'and everything's absolutely delicious. These are the best roast potatoes I've ever had.'

'I beat them up,' Robbie said.

'Pardon?' Millie said.

'After boiling them, I beat them up in the pan.'

'It helps to make them fluffy and crisp,' Niall explained.

'Ah!' Millie said. 'Well, I must remember that little trick.'

They ate in silence for a little while with just the occasional sigh of appreciation at the good food and, at the end, Robbie cleared the plates away, taking Millie's from her like the perfect waiter.

A moment later, Niall served the Christmas pudding dancing with flames.

'What a treat!' Millie exclaimed from the sofa.

'And we have cream too,' Robbie said.

The boys joined Millie in the living room and they all tucked in to generous portions of Christmas pudding in front of the wood burner.

'I can't remember when I enjoyed a real Christmas dinner like this,' Millie said.

Niall looked at her in surprise. 'Don't you usually have one?'

Millie gave a self-conscious little shrug. 'James and I used to go away – usually abroad – so we didn't really do the whole Christmas thing. I'm not really sure why now. I think we were just being a bit rebellious by going swimming and eating a pizza.'

'Cool!' Robbie said. 'Can we do that one Christmas, Dad?'

'Certainly not,' Niall said.

'No, I wouldn't recommend it,' Millie said. 'I've really missed this. Thanks so much, Niall. And Robbie.'

'You're very welcome,' Niall said.

For a while, they sat together watching the fire and gazing at the Christmas tree whilst Robbie read one of his comics.

'I suppose I should get some more wood in,' Niall said, getting up at last and taking the empty bowls into the kitchen before leaving the cottage.

'Do you *really* never celebrate Christmas?' Robbie asked once his father was out of earshot.

'I'm afraid I don't,' Millie said. 'Isn't that silly of me?'

Robbie nodded and Millie laughed. 'I've never met anyone who doesn't like it,' he said.

'Oh, I like it,' Millie said. 'I *love* it! But it's different if you spend it on your own.'

'That must be sad.'

'It is. It was,' Millie said, remembering the Christmases that James would spend with his family. Not once had he invited her to join them.

'You wouldn't enjoy it anyway,' James had told her with a laugh but she would have liked to have been given the opportunity to make her own mind up about what she did and didn't enjoy.

'But I had some brilliant Christmases growing up with my family,' she said, steering the conversation in a more cheerful direction. 'We always played lots of silly games and ate much too much food.'

Robbie watched her as she spoke and Millie was encouraged to go on, telling him about her two brothers, Marcus and Jake, and the antics they used to get up to.

'It's snowing again, Millie,' Robbie said as she finished telling him about the time an eight year old Jake had chased her into a muck heap and got into terrible trouble with their mother.

'Let me see,' Millie said, hobbling across to the window and looking out. What was it about snow that was so magical, she wondered as she looked up into the myriad flakes that were spiralling down from the heavens? It visited the UK almost every year, sometimes for months at a time, and yet the first fall never failed to entrance even though it was bound to cause chaos. Nothing was so awe-inspiring as beautiful big fluffy snowflakes falling out of a pewter-coloured sky.

'I'll have to show you the cave sometime,' Millie said, suddenly remembering a time when she'd been sheltering from the rain in the cave on one of her family holidays.

'The cave?' Robbie said, his bright eyes widening.

Millie nodded. 'I think I was about your age when I first saw it,' she told him. 'I couldn't believe what I'd found. It seemed to stretch back for miles but I don't think it does really. It just seemed like that at the time.' She smiled at the memory. 'My brothers were so mad that I'd been the one to find it and I insisted that they called it

"Millie's Cave".'

'And did they?'

'No,' she said. 'Of course not but I knew it was mine all the same.'

'Where is it?' Robbie asked.

'You know where we were walking today – where I slipped? It's just a bit further along the beach. Perhaps we can go and look for it if it stops snowing. I'm sure my ankle's feeling better.'

It was then that Niall returned with a pile of logs in his arms.

'Boy, it's cold out there now,' he said as he placed logs in the basket by the fireplace.

'Can I go outside?' Robbie asked.

'I don't want you going too far,' Niall told him as he took his hat and coat off.

'I won't,' Robbie said. 'I just want to build a snowman.'

'Okay then,' Niall said, 'but wrap up warm and no throwing snowballs at the windows.' Robbie rolled his eyes and Millie looked across at Niall who shook his head. 'We once had an incident with a very large snowball and a very small leaded window.'

'Ah!' Millie said. 'I'm sure it was an accident. He's such a great kid. You must be so proud of him.'

Niall nodded and watched as his son – who was now decked out in coat, hat, scarf and gloves – began the long cold process of making a snowman. 'I am,' he said, 'and I don't know what I would have done without him these last two years.'

Millie looked at him and once again saw the shadows of sadness cross his face.

'He must have been a great comfort to you,' she said.

Niall closed his eyes for a moment and then turned his back on the window and looked at Millie. 'When Emma died, I didn't know what to do with myself. I was like a spare part just floating around and I had this crazy temptation to ring her mobile number. The digits just kept flying through my head as if they were taunting me. So, one day, I did ring it.' He gave a hollow laugh. 'What did I think would happen? That she'd answer and say it had all been a mistake and that she was alive? Did I think she'd laugh and call me a silly boy in the way she always did?'

'Oh, Niall,' Millie said in a half whisper.

'Without Robbie, I might have gone completely mad but I had to be strong for him and he was strong for me and, somehow, we got through.' He sat down in the chair beside the wood burner and the two of them gazed into the brilliant orange flames.

'I never thought I'd enjoy a real fire so much,' Niall said.

'Do you have a fireplace at Bathwick?'

He shook his head. 'It's all boarded up but I'm very tempted to open it up now.'

They watched the flames dancing for a few more minutes before Niall got up and walked across to the window.

'Where's Robbie?' he said. 'I can't see him.'

'Isn't he building his snowman?' Millie asked.

'No. He's not,' Niall said, moving towards the door at lightning speed.

Millie listened from her home on the sofa as Niall opened and closed the front door of the cottage. She could hear him calling Robbie's name and then, a few minutes later, he returned.

'Millie!' he said, sounding a little out of breath. 'I can't see him anywhere.'

'Oh, god!' Millie suddenly exclaimed, her face paling. 'I think I know where he might be.'

'Where?' Niall said, the panic obvious in the one abrupt word.

'I told him about the cave.'

'What cave?'

'The cave along the beach. You don't think he's gone there, do you?'

'But the tide will be coming in and it's getting dark already.'

Millie stared at Niall as he sprang into action.

'You're not going anywhere on that ankle of yours,' Niall told her as he saw her struggling to get off the sofa.

'Well, I'm not sitting here like a useless lump if Robbie's in danger,' she said.

They were both outside in hats, coats and boots in less than a minute. The air was bitterly cold as they left the cosy warmth of the cottage and the wind took their breaths away. The snow was still falling and they were able to trace Robbie's footprints which, unsurprisingly, led down to the beach.

'Robbie! ROBBIE!' Niall shouted across the beach but the wind took his words before they'd travelled far. The little boy was nowhere to be seen.

Millie couldn't help feeling responsible. She should never have told Robbie about the cave. But how was she to know that he'd take himself off there? She shook her head in anger at herself. Of *course* he was going to venture out there. He was a boy.

'Where is it, Millie?' Niall shouted at her above the wind a few minutes later.

'A bit further – just passed those rocks,' she said as she desperately tried to keep up with him on her painful ankle.

At last, they reached the rocky part of the beach where the dark cliffs soared up into the sky. The tide was coming in at an alarming rate and Millie worried that the cave might already be cut off.

As they reached the entrance, their eyes adjusting to the darkness, they saw the tiny figure of Robbie.

'ROBS!' Niall shouted.

'DAD!' Robbie shouted back and Millie watched as Niall waded through the icy water to where Robbie was perched on a boulder. As he reached his son, he was waist deep in the water which boiled around his body in cold, icy waves.

Millie watched from the entrance to the cave where she'd managed to clamber onto a rock to get out of the rising water. Niall was holding his arms out towards Robbie who launched himself into them.

'Hold tight!' Niall said as he turned around with his son in his arms and began to wade through the water out of the cave.

'Robbie!' Millie cried. 'We were so worried. Are you all right?'

Robbie nodded but his eyes were closing.

'We've got to get him back quickly,' Niall said. 'He's frozen.'

It was a strange, surreal walk back to the cottage where time seemed to slow down and speed up all at once. The wind whipped the snow around their faces and the sky was darkening fast. All the time, Niall kept talking to Robbie, making sure he was conscious.

It was such a blessed relief to get back inside and Niall placed Robbie in front of the wood burner, quickly stripping him of his wet clothes and rubbing him down with a blanket, paying particular attention to his head.

'Millie – can you make him a hot drink? A Ribena would be perfect.'

'Of course,' she said, taking her own wet things off and moving into the kitchen.

She was back with the Ribena a moment later.

'Robbie – can you cough for me?' Robbie gave a little cough and Niall took the hot drink from Millie and supervised his son drinking it.

'What was the coughing about?' Millie asked.

'To make sure he can swallow safely,' Niall said.

'Is he all right?'

'I think he's in shock,' Niall said.

It was then that Millie noticed Niall was still wearing his wet things.

'You've got to get out of those,' she said. 'You're absolutely soaked.'

Niall nodded. His face was pale. 'Okay,' he said.

'I'll take care of Robbie,' she said, wrapping her arms around the boy in the hope of imparting some of her own body heat to him. 'You're okay, Robbie,' she said over and over to him like a chant. 'You're okay.'

Millie wasn't sure how long they sat there together in front of the wood burner but when Niall walked back into the room, she noticed that he had changed his clothes and was rubbing his hair with a towel.

'How is he?' he asked, kneeling down on the floor beside them both.

'I think he's sleepy,' Millie said.

'I'll take him to my room. He should be okay now,' Niall said, scooping his son up into his arms for the second time that day and heading upstairs. When he returned, he flopped into the chair by the fireplace.

'Let me get you a hot drink,' Millie said. Niall simply nodded.

Millie made him a cup of tea. Strong. Milk. No sugar. That's how he liked it.

'I'm so sorry,' she said to him a moment later as she handed him the hot drink. 'I feel just awful.'

'It's not your fault,' Niall told her.

'But it was me who told him about the cave.'

'It doesn't matter – he would have found it sooner or later,' Niall said. 'He's a boy, remember? Boys like getting into trouble. It's in their genes.'

'I'd make a *terrible* mother!' she said.

'You'd make a *brilliant* mother,' he said. 'I'm sure your brothers used to get into all sorts of scrapes, didn't they?'

Millie nodded, remembering the time that Marcus had taken a tumble out of a tree, and when Jake had fallen off his bike as he'd been trying to ride it with no hands over a ramp.

'Boys will be boys,' Niall said, 'and – whilst we don't want them to kill themselves as they explore the world – we've got to give them space to find their own way.'

'You're being incredibly calm about all this,' Millie told him.

He sighed. 'The shock will probably hit me in the middle of the night and I'll wake up screaming. I apologise in advance.'

'I'll be ready with the whisky.'

'Thank you,' he said and he grinned.

'This is one Christmas I won't forget in a hurry,' she told him.

'Not for all the wrong reasons, I hope,' he said. 'Hey – how's your ankle?'

'It hurts like hell,' Millie said, 'but I'd kind of forgotten about it until you asked.'

'Get back on the sofa, you,' he said.

'Doctor's orders?'

'Absolutely.'

Millie sat down on the sofa before stretching her legs out on it.

'He'll be all right, won't he?' she asked Niall.

He nodded. 'We came pretty close there for a minute. Thank goodness you knew where he'd gone.'

Millie swallowed hard. 'I wish I hadn't told him about–'

'You don't need to keep apologising,' Niall interrupted her. 'You weren't to know what would happen.'

'But I should have thought things through.'

Niall shook his head. 'He's okay. That's the main thing.' He closed his eyes for a moment.

'You okay?' Millie asked.

'I was watching him fall asleep upstairs,' he said, shaking his head. 'Sometimes, he looks *so* much like Emma that it hurts.'

'He looks like you too,' Millie said softly.

'You think?'

'Absolutely. He's a really handsome boy,' Millie said and then bit her lip as she realised what she'd said.

Niall gazed across the room at her and their eyes locked for a moment before Millie looked away, a blush colouring her cheeks.

A little cry came from upstairs and Niall was on his feet in an instant.

'Robbie?' He motioned to Millie to stay where she was and left the room. Millie stayed put on the sofa and listened to the distant murmurs of Niall talking to his son. She couldn't make out the words but they were slow and low and deeply comforting and, with the heat from the stove and the exhaustion she felt, she found herself drifting off to sleep.

She wasn't sure how long she'd been asleep but, when she woke up, the curtains had been drawn and Niall was in the kitchen.

'Vegetable soup okay?' he asked.

Millie yawned and nodded. 'What time is it?'

'After eight,' he said.

'Really?' Millie was up and on her feet before she could think. 'Ouch!' she said. 'I forgot.'

'Sit back down,' he said. 'I'll come to you.'

'How's Robbie?'

'He's asleep again. I sat with him for a while until he went back to sleep.' He placed the bowls of soup on the coffee table between them.

'Niall?' Millie said a few minutes later when they were finishing the soup.

'Yes?'

Millie wasn't quite sure what she wanted to say but there was something about the intimacy of the room with the stove roaring and the thick curtains drawn against the winter night that felt like a confessional.

'I've really loved being here with you and Robbie this Christmas. I can't think when I've enjoyed a Christmas more and,' she paused, awkwardness preventing her from going on for a moment, 'well, I'm not sure what's going through my auntie's head but I just wanted you to know that–' She stopped.

'It's okay,' Niall said, crossing the room and sitting on the sofa with her.

'I just wanted to say–' but, before the words were out – before she could tell him how she felt about him, he'd leaned forward, his lips gently brushing hers in a warm kiss that made her feel strange and wonderful all at once.

'Is that what you wanted to say?' he asked her a moment later.

Millie smiled. 'I think it might have been,' she said.

'That's a relief,' he said, 'because I've been wanting to say it too.'

'Really?' she said, her eyes widening in surprise.

He nodded and grinned. 'Even before your aunt's presents.'

Millie looked at him in disbelief. 'But I worried that you might think it's too early, you know?' she said as his hands found hers and held them.

'It isn't too early,' he said and he leaned forward to kiss her again.

'I don't want Christmas to end,' she whispered.

'Neither do I,' he said. 'I never thought I'd enjoy another Christmas ever again after I lost Emma but life really does go on, doesn't it? In its weird and wonderful way.'

'Are you saying I'm weird?' Millie teased.

'No, I'm saying you're wonderful,' he told her.

'Goodness,' she said. 'I never expected this to happen. I came here to get away from everything.'

'Me too,' he said.

'I guess that fate had other plans,' she said.

'Or your Aunt Louise,' he said.

Millie sighed. 'Just wait until I see her.'

Niall squeezed her hands. 'You won't be too hard on her will you? I mean, if she did send us both here on purpose – which I'm not entirely sure she did – it was with the very best of intentions, wasn't it? And she didn't get it completely wrong, did she?'

A small smile began to spread across Millie's face. 'No,' she said. 'She didn't get it completely wrong at all.'

CHAPTER 8

The snow continued to fall the next day and didn't stop until after lunch. Then, the three of them left the cottage and, with careful feet encased in wellies, made their way down to the beach. Nobody spoke as they walked through a world in which the only sound came from the distant roar of the sea. It was as if each of them was trying to memorise the moment in an attempt to capture it forever: the muted winter colours of black, grey and white, the icy freshness of the wind on their faces, and the salt-laden air which they could taste on their lips.

The sand was still frozen and covered in a good layer of snow. How beautiful it looked, Millie thought, and how she was going to miss it when she left tomorrow.

'You're thinking about leaving, aren't you?' Niall said.

Millie nodded. 'It's hard to live in the present when the future is pressing down upon you, isn't it?'

Niall sighed. 'Do you *have* to go?'

'I do,' she said. 'They're expecting me back at work.'

'I wish you'd stay until the New Year.'

'I wish I could too.'

They walked the length of the beach. Robbie stayed in sight this time, perhaps more conscious of the dangers of the place now than he had been the day before. Occasionally, he would turn to look back, just to make sure they were still there.

'It's okay,' Robbie said at one point.

'What's okay?' Niall asked.

'It's okay if you hold hands,' he told them with a little smile before turning his attention to a frozen rock pool.

Millie looked at Niall and they both laughed.

'How did he know?' Millie whispered.

Niall grinned. 'Well, I might have told him I liked you.'

'What? *When?*' Millie asked in surprise.

'When he was trying to get to sleep last night,' he confessed. 'I just asked him how he felt about me liking you.'

'But you hadn't told *me* by then,' Millie pointed out.

'I know,' he said, 'but I was on the verge of telling you.'

Millie smiled as a huge bubble of happiness rose up inside her and Niall held out his hand towards her and, knowing that she had Robbie's blessing, she took it.

When they got back, they cobbled together a jolly lunch of all the bits and pieces that had been left over from Christmas and then they sprawled out in front of the wood burner and watched a light-hearted film together on the tiny old television as the light faded from the sky.

The evening was spent playing games, reading books and telling each other silly stories from their pasts and Millie couldn't help feeling how natural everything was. Nothing was forced. They were three people who liked each other's company and Millie dared to dream that during that Christmas, she had had a tiny glimpse of what her future might be.

But the future had to be put on hold because, the next day, Millie had to leave.

'Can't you ring in sick?' Robbie asked as they helped her put her things into her car. 'Dad could write you a sick note.'

'I could, you know,' he said with a grin.

Millie laughed. 'That is very tempting,' she said. She had truly never felt sadder to leave Cove Cottage than she did that morning and there had been some pretty tearful departures in the past at the end of school holidays.

The track to the cottage would have been impossible for her to drive up in her little car now that it was covered in snow so Niall towed her up, stopping once they had reached the main road.

'Give me a call if you run into any problems,' he told her after disconnecting the tow rope. 'I'm not sure what the roads are like but I'd avoid the ones over Exmoor.'

'I bet it looks beautiful,' Millie said, getting out of the car to say goodbye.

'I think its beauty would start to exasperate after a few hours of being stuck in a cold car,' he said.

'Good point,' she said. 'I'll stick to the major roads.'

'How's your ankle?'

'Much better,' she told him. 'I'm just glad it isn't my right one for driving. Thanks for taking such good care of me, Dr Darby.'

He laughed and they stood staring at one another for a moment, the icy air swirling about them.

'It's been–'

'I've had–'

They both said at once and then laughed.

'I just wanted to say that I never want to spend Christmas any other way,' he said.

She smiled. 'So, same time next year?'

Niall frowned. 'I hope I get to see you before then,' he said.

'Oh, you will,' she told him, crossing the space between them and kissing him full on the mouth.

Robbie, who had accompanied his father in the four-wheel-drive, got out of the car now.

'Bye, Robbie,' Millie said.

His young face was full of sadness for a moment but then he gave a smile which seemed to light up the whole world and he raced towards Millie and hugged her.

'Don't set me off now!' she said, blinking her tears away.

'I don't want you to go,' he told her, his voice muffled as his face was pressed into her winter coat.

'But we're going to see each other again soon,' she told him, her fingers stroking his dark hair.

He looked up at her. 'Promise?'

'Promise,' she told him.

Niall stepped forward. 'Somebody once told me about the power of a group hug,' he said. 'It's something I've never tried before.' With that, he put his arms around both Robbie and Millie.

'What you think?' Millie asked him a moment later. 'Any good?'

Niall took a deep breath. 'It's just about perfect, I'd say.'

EPILOGUE – ONE WEEK EARLIER

'You're making excellent progress, Mrs Chambers. I'm very pleased with you.'

Louise Chambers gave a little laugh. 'And I've been very pleased with you, Doctor Eastwood!'

He smiled and she couldn't help thinking – once again – how very handsome he was. Such a charming young man. If only she was a few years – a few *decades* younger. Say about the same age as her great niece, Millie. Then, she thought, Doctor Eastwood would be in trouble.

'And what are you doing for Christmas, Doctor Eastwood?' she asked him as she rolled the sleeve of her cardigan down.

He sighed. 'Trying to get through it as quickly and quietly as possible.'

'Oh?'

'Christmas is always a difficult time,' he said, nodding to a silver-framed photograph of his late wife on his desk.

'Ah, yes, of course,' Louise said. 'You know, I've got a rather lovely cottage out on the Devon coast?'

'Oh, right?'

'It's used as a holiday let but it's empty this Christmas. I think the threat of bad weather has put people off. Anyway, you're more than welcome to use it. Take young Robbie with you and have yourself a proper break away from everything.'

'Really?' Dr Eastwood said in surprise.

'*Absolutely*,' Louise said. 'Now, I'll give you a call this evening with all the details. Okay?'

That evening, after the promised call to Dr Eastwood, Louise rang her great niece.

'Millie? It's your Aunt Louise here. Now, didn't you say you wanted to stay at the cottage sometime? Well, it's standing empty over Christmas...'

51

Christmas at the Castle

To my lovely readers. Wishing you all a Merry Christmas!

Thank you to Bella and her beautiful Scottish deerhounds who helped to inspire Bagpipe, to Sam Jarvis who is simply a marvel, to Catriona for helping me polish this novella and for letting me use her name too, and to Roy for being Roy!

CHAPTER 1

'I just don't see why we have to spend Christmas in the coldest, dampest part of the castle!' Fiona complained.

Catriona Fraser sighed as she saw the exasperation on her fifteen-year old daughter's face.

'I've told you, Fee' she began, 'the MacNeices have hired part of the castle for the Christmas holidays and you know how much we're able to make from that. I couldn't afford to say no.'

'So you stick your own children in the dungeon,' Fiona said, flicking a strand of her long red hair over her shoulder. She was going through a dramatic stage where everything in her life was a tragedy. She'd make a really fine actress one day, Catriona couldn't help thinking.

'It's not a dungeon,' Catriona said patiently as she dried the dishes on the draining board and put them away. 'You've got your own bedroom—'

'It's pokey.'

'It's not pokey. Well, only in comparison to what you're used to, but I want the MacNeices to have the whole of that floor,' Catriona acceded, 'and you've got one of the best views of the loch from your room in the east wing.'

'I hate that wing,' Fiona said. 'It makes me feel jumpy.'

Catriona frowned. 'What do you mean?'

'It's all dark and depressing.'

'Well, hopefully, we can give it a lick of paint in the New Year – what do you think?'

'It's not before time,' Fiona said.

'And, in the meantime, we've got one of the castle's best fireplaces in the living room there. We'll make it nice and cosy, eh?'

Fiona didn't look convinced. 'I'd rather have Christmas in the Great Hall.'

'I know, darling, but we can't this year.'

'We always have Christmas there. What would Daddy think about us not spending Christmas there?'

Catriona flinched. Her daughter really knew how to push her

57

buttons, didn't she?

'I'm sure he'd understand,' she said, desperately trying to remain calm as she thought of the husband she'd lost just two years ago. 'Anyway it's not for forever.'

'No, just for the most important time of year.'

Catriona watched as her daughter stomped out of the room and then she released the sigh she'd been holding in. It was an impossible situation, she thought. If she didn't let out the rooms during the holidays, they wouldn't be able to live in the castle at all and she didn't want to think of what the alternative might be. But it was never a popular choice with her children.

Caldoon Castle had belonged to her husband's family and she was determined to keep it going and hand it on to her children, but the castle wouldn't be in one piece to hand on if they didn't make sacrifices in the short term. It was hard on Fiona and Brody, she knew that. At fifteen and ten respectively, her children were of an age when they valued their privacy and Fiona in particular didn't take well to strangers invading their home.

Perhaps she'd sheltered them too much from the outside world, she thought, not for the first time. Living in the middle of nowhere, twelve miles from the nearest town, wasn't easy for youngsters growing up. Then there'd been the decision three years ago to home tutor them when their father had become ill. The long commute to the nearest schools had been one less thing to worry about as she'd nursed Andrew and he'd wanted to have them near him too.

Catriona picked up the photo of her and Andrew which stood on the kitchen dresser. It had been taken the summer after their wedding twenty years ago when he'd brought her home to Caldoon Castle.

'You'll love it,' he'd told her and Catriona had believed him, remembering the first time they'd driven up the long winding track which led to the castle. She could still recall the sense of awe and anticipation she'd felt when she'd seen the five-storey tower shooting into the perfect blue sky and the view from the top over the loch had taken her breath away. Those feelings hadn't diminished over the years. Every time she drove up the pot-hole strewn track and got her first glimpse of the castle, it made her gasp.

'All this belongs to your family?' she'd asked Andrew that day – once she'd finally been able to speak.

'Eight generations,' he'd said.

Catriona didn't even know where her grandparents had lived let alone anyone further back than that. She'd led a simple, non-exciting life in the village of Lochnabrae on the other side of the town of Strathcorrie. She was an only child and had lived with her parents in a modest white-washed cottage. Never in her wildest dreams had she imagined living in a castle. But then she'd met Andrew at a ceilidh and he'd whisked her to within an inch of her life across the dance floor and she'd fallen madly in love.

'I'm hoping you'll be as happy here as I've been,' he'd said when he'd brought her to his family home for the first time. And Catriona had been so sure that she would be but she hadn't banked on losing Andrew.

She closed her eyes as she remembered those last few painful days as her husband had slipped away from her. The cancer had been shockingly swift and had left a huge void in their lives that would never be filled. Catriona had done her best to work her way through her own grief whilst comforting Fee and Brody, and the dark relentless days after they'd lost Andrew had slowly become a little less bleak and a little more bearable.

She replaced the photograph on the dresser just as Brody walked into the kitchen.

'Fee's in a strop. *Again!*'

'She's okay,' Catriona said.

'Seriously, Mom, you need to deal with her before she gets outta hand.'

'Pardon?' Catriona said. 'Brody – just *how* many US TV series are you watching at the moment?'

He shrugged. 'Three or four.'

'I'm going to have to stop you. You're beginning to sound like a gangster and you've *got* to stop calling me "Mom"!'

Brody tutted and rolled his eyes in a manner which looked so like his late father. He had the same rich chestnut-coloured hair too.

'Have you done your homework?' she asked him.

'Yup!'

'Can I see it?'

'I thought we'd broken up for the holiday, *Mum*,' he said, stressing the Anglicised pronunciation.

She nodded. Brody was right. But it was sometimes hard to switch from being her children's teacher to being their mum when both school and home were in the same place.

'As long as it's done,' she said. 'You wouldn't want it hanging over you all Christmas, would you?'

He shook his head but she could tell that his mind wasn't on homework.

'They're in the tin on the table,' she said with a grin, watching as he made a beeline for the chocolate cookies she'd made earlier. 'No more than two!'

'Aw, Mum!'

'I mean it.' She watched as he fished around in the tin for the two biggest cookies he could find. 'Brody?'

'Yeah?'

'How do you feel about us having people to stay here at Christmas? I know we've only ever done summer and Easter holidays before.'

He shrugged. 'Okay, s'pose.'

'You don't mind too much about us not using the Great Hall?'

'Nah,' he said. 'Not since Goliath moved in.'

Catriona smiled. Goliath was the name of the spider that had made his home next to the woodpile by the Great Hall fireplace. Catriona was lucky that she wasn't afraid of spiders but her husband had been, which was a serious handicap to owning a fifteenth-century castle, and he seemed to have passed on his fear to both of his children.

'We'll make the living room in the east wing nice and cosy,' she said.

'I know,' he said with a grin that made her feel a little bit better.

'Do you want to take a hot water bottle up with you to keep your hands warm?'

'I'm not a girl, Mum!'

'I know,' she said, 'but I don't want you getting cold in that bedroom of yours.'

'It's not too bad,' he said.

'Well, let me know if you do get cold, won't you?'

He nodded again. 'I'll let you know as soon as I can see my breath!' He stuffed a cookie into his mouth as he left the room.

Caldoon Castle was a blissful place to live in the summer months but it wasn't such a friendly place in the winter, Catriona thought, and they'd had their fair share of snowdrifts, frozen pipes and broken boilers in the past.

Now, sitting in the kitchen next to the old range which was the warmest place in the whole castle, Catriona wondered – not for the first time – what was to become of them all.

CHAPTER 2

Iain MacNeice had finished work only two hours late on that final Friday before the Christmas holidays, which was a small miracle really considering they'd been closing the deal on the Manders account. He had a thumping headache as he left the advertising agency, walking out into the cold Edinburgh air. His secretary, Janice, had stayed on to help him clear all the paperwork and had asked if he wanted her to call a taxi but he'd declined. He wanted to walk. He *needed* to walk. And so he'd taken the well-known route from his office off Princes Street to his home in one of the Georgian crescents of the New Town.

As a student in Edinburgh, Iain had known that he'd never return to the little Highland village he'd grown up in. He'd fallen completely in love with the magical capital city and had never left.

Striding through the dark streets, the street lamps and the lights from the large sash windows of the Georgian terraces guiding his way, he realised that he was happy to leave his work behind him for the next couple of weeks. He couldn't remember when he'd last taken more than a few days' holiday. His two daughters, Lexi and Chrissa, were always reminding him but the expansion of his company had meant sacrificing time with his family. Time which had already contributed to the breakdown of his marriage.

For a moment, he thought about Dawn, his wife of twenty-two years, who was now living in Los Angeles with her new partner who did something wildly exciting in the film industry. It was a world away from his tame existence in an advertising firm in Edinburgh, that was for sure. He'd seen the photos his daughters had taken of the white-washed mansion high up in Beverly Hills with an infinity pool and Jacuzzi. The place looked more like a hotel than a home but Lexi and Chrissa were of an age when that kind of thing impressed them – more so than the comparatively modest city apartment they shared together in Edinburgh.

As he turned into the crescent, his feet slipping on the icy pavement, he looked up at the first floor family home. The curtains hadn't yet been drawn and he glimpsed the enormous Christmas tree

62

which he'd ordered. The delivery men had had quite a struggle getting it up the stairs but it looked wonderful with its red and gold baubles and star-shaped lights and Iain had made sure that there were heaps of presents to open underneath it. Of course, they'd have to take the presents with them when they left for their holiday in the Highlands the next morning.

Entering the communal hallway now, and walking up the stairs to the first floor, he couldn't help feeling a little anxious about the days that lay ahead. He knew he'd been somewhat lacking as a father in recent years, spending long periods away from home and not spending nearly enough time with his daughters. But that really couldn't be helped, could it? A man had to work and save for his family, and his wife had quickly got used to buying the best of everything for herself, her daughters and her home. And, for a while, Iain had liked that lifestyle too but he couldn't help feeling that there was something missing from his life: something fundamental that money couldn't buy.

Reaching inside his pocket he found his key and opened the door.

'Mrs Crompton? I'm home!' he called. A moment later, a stout lady appeared.

'You're late,' she said, her eyes narrowing at the sight of him.

'I know,' Iain said, feeling thoroughly chastised by those two little words. 'Did Janice not call you to explain?'

'Aye, she did,' Mrs Crompton said, untying the pinafore she wore and folding it neatly before grabbing her coat from a hook in the hallway. 'My Murray hasn't had his tea yet.'

'I haven't had mine,' Iain said, giving her a little grin that he hoped might appease her.

'Yes, well, that's your own doing now, isn't it?'

'I suppose it is,' he said, taking off his coat and hanging it up.

'I won't always be here, you know,' Mrs Crompton went on as she picked up her large holdall-style handbag. 'Got my health to think about. I can't be bending down picking up other people's rubbish my whole life, you know. Got my poor knees to think about.'

Iain nodded. Mrs Crompton had been saying those words every day since he'd hired her three years ago but, miraculously, her knees had been holding out.

'Well, thank you for holding the fort here,' he said, 'and I've got something for you.' He walked over to a table in the hallway and opened a drawer, taking out an envelope. 'A little something for the Christmas holidays.'

She pursed up her mouth and, for a moment, he thought he was about to hear a thank you but she simply nodded and put the envelope in her handbag before putting on her coat, pulling her hat onto her head and leaving.

Iain stood in the hallway feeling stunned. He was the director of his own global company, responsible for over fifty members of staff and in charge of making important decisions every hour of his working day and yet he'd just been made to feel like a naughty little boy in his own home.

'How does she do it?' he said to his reflection in the mirror above the table as he dropped his keys into a bowl. His dark eyes looked red and his skin looked as if it could do with a good dose of sunshine. In short, he looked run down. He shook his head. It was the start of the Christmas holidays and he was determined not to feel sorry for himself.

'Girls?' he called, wondering where his daughters were. He stood silently listening for clues and could hear a strange, monotonous thudding sound coming from Lexi's room. He approached with caution. At sixteen, Lexi was ferociously private and woe betide anybody who entered without knocking. And so Iain knocked, tentatively at first and then with a firm fist when it became apparent that she couldn't hear him.

'What?' her voice came from within.

'It's Dad,' Iain said, opening the door a crack. Lexi was lying on her side on her bed, her long dark hair cascading over her shoulders. She was flipping though a magazine and Chrissa, Iain's eight-year-old, was sitting on the floor.

'Hi, Dad,' Chrissa said, getting up to give him a hug.

'Hey, sweetheart,' he said, kissing her forehead which smelled of the raspberry shampoo she loved so much. She was in her pyjamas and looked all cosy, warm and snuggly and he just wanted to hug her for the rest of the evening. The same couldn't be said about Lexi who hadn't even looked up as he'd walked into her room.

'Okay, Lex?' he asked as he turned the music down causing her to scowl at him. 'Good last day at school.'

'The usual,' she muttered.

'Right,' Iain said, wishing he knew what she meant by that but she rarely let him glimpse into her world. He was resolutely locked out of it. 'Have you two eaten?' he asked, steering the conversation on to safer territory.

'We ate *hours* ago, Dad,' Lexi said, finally glancing up at him, her eyes full of scorn at his question.

'Oh. I was going to call out for a pizza,' he said.

'I'm stuffed,' Chrissa said. 'Mrs Crompton made this funny fish dish.'

'Was it nice?' he asked.

'It was filling,' Chrissa said diplomatically. 'She didn't leave any for you. She said you shouldn't be so late and she put your portion in a plastic tub to take home to Mr Crompton.'

Iain nodded. That sounded about right, he thought.

'Well,' he said, clapping his hands together, 'who wants to see what I've brought home?'

'More presents?' Chrissa said, her eyes lighting up.

'I thought we'd have a little present opening to mark the beginning of the holidays. I ran into Jenners at lunchtime today,' he said.

'You mean you actually chose us presents *yourself* and didn't get your secretary to buy them for you?' Lexi said.

Iain frowned. 'Now why would you say something like that?'

'Because it's true, isn't it? Mum always said you never had time to choose things yourself.'

'Oh, did she?'

Lexi nodded, her eyes fixed on a photo of some boy band in her magazine.

Iain sighed. His ex-wife had done a pretty good hatchet job on him, hadn't she? They'd been separated for three years now and she was still bad mouthing him to their daughters. It was one of the reasons he got nervous every time they went to stay with her in LA. Even though she seemed happily settled with her new partner, Dawn still couldn't stop herself from painting him black. Mind you, Lexi's accusation was true. Iain had been known to hand over present-buying duties to Janice but that wasn't because he was too lazy or couldn't be bothered to choose gifts himself. If anything, it was because he cared about his girls so much and wanted to be sure – to be *absolutely* sure – that he got the very best presents for his girls and Janice had two daughters of her own and always knew what to get.

Whenever he'd tried to choose something himself, it always seemed to go wrong, like the time he'd bought wildly expensive tickets to wrong pop group for Lexi.

'That group is so lame!' she'd complained. He'd given the tickets to Janice's daughters who'd been much more appreciative and had given Lexi a very safe gift voucher instead.

Now, however, he was quite sure he'd made the right choice and he reached into the pocket of his suit jacket and removed two tiny packages wrapped in silver paper with red bows exquisitely tied around them. He handed the first to Chrissa and the second to Lexi who deigned to put down her magazine.

He watched as the girls ripped off the paper and opened the boxes at the same time to reveal identical silver lockets.

'Wow!' Chrissa cried. 'It's so pretty, Daddy. Thank you!' She launched herself at him, fixing her arms around his waist.

'You're welcome, darling.'

'Can I put it on?'

'Just for a minute but make sure you don't sleep wearing it, okay?' He turned to Lexi who had opened the locket and was looking inside.

'It's empty,' she said.

'Of course,' he said as he sat down on the bed next to her. 'It's for you to fill. You choose which photos you want to put in there.' He waited a moment, hoping to hear some sort of contented response from her but none was forthcoming. 'Do you like it?'

She nodded.

'Good,' he said and that was it: the sum total of her response. 'Are you two packed and ready for tomorrow? We'll be leaving straight after breakfast.'

Chrissa nodded. 'I've got *everything* ready,' she said.

'Good. Lexi?'

'Do we have to go? I want to stay at Mum's for Christmas. We *always* do that,' Lexi said.

'Which is precisely why you're *not* doing that this year,' Iain told his daughter. 'It's my turn to spend time with you and we're doing something different and you're going to enjoy it.'

'I won't,' she said.

'How can you possibly know that?'

'I just do,' she said with the logic of a teenager.

'It's not everyone who gets to stay in a medieval castle for

Christmas,' Iain said.

'Lucky them,' she said.

Iain sighed and got up off the bed. 'Don't stay up too late now, will you? And time for your bed, Chrissa,' he said, leading his younger daughter out of the room.

'Daddy?' she said.

'Yes?'

'Will Mummy be coming to the castle too?'

'Darling, you know she won't.'

'But she might surprise us.'

'I seriously doubt that and you mustn't build your hopes up either.'

'I think she'll come,' Chrissa said as they entered her bedroom which was a symphony of pink.

'You brushed your teeth?' he asked, deciding it was probably best not to continue with the subject of her mother and whether or not she was going to visit.

'Of course,' Chrissa said like a grown-up.

'Good. And don't forget to take your necklace off.'

He watched as she did so, placing it carefully on the bedside table before climbing into bed with her favourite soft toy which had lost so many parts over the years that Iain wasn't quite sure what it was anymore. He tucked her in and bent to kiss her soft rosy cheek, inhaling her raspberry sweetness.

'Daddy?' she said.

'What is it, darling?'

'Do you want Mummy to spend Christmas with us?'

The question was so unexpected that he felt truly stumped. He straightened up, moving away from the bed and only turning around to face Chrissa once he was at the door.

'I think you'd better get some sleep,' he said, leaving the room before she could say anything else.

Lexi's light would remain on until at least eleven o'clock. He'd kind of given up that particular battle. He walked through to the living room. The Christmas tree was all lit up and looking lovely if lonely now that he was the only one present to enjoy it.

Iain collapsed onto the sofa and rubbed his sore eyes. He had to admit to being very anxious about the holiday which lay ahead. Was it really a good idea to hole up in a draughty old castle with two daughters he hardly knew, especially when they'd probably both rather be with their mother soaking up the Californian sunshine?

He sighed. How did he get himself into these situations? Did this happen to all parents around the world or was he just really unlucky? For a second, he thought about pouring himself a whisky but concluded that a cup of tea was probably a safer, saner option especially as his headache hadn't cleared yet.

As he headed into the kitchen, the sound of a thumping bass was heard from Lexi's room. He could go back through and tell her to turn it down or even tell her to turn it off as it was pretty late now, but he knew how that conversation would pan out and, luckily, Chrissa seemed able to sleep through anything.

Abandoning the kitchen and any thought of dinner, he headed back to the living room and walked straight to the drinks cabinet where he poured himself a very small whisky.

Things would be better in the morning, wouldn't they?

CHAPTER 3

Things weren't any better in the morning. If anything, they were worse. Chrissa had her little pink suitcase packed and was ready for action but Lexi was dragging her heels.

'I've got to wash my hair,' she said.

'Lexi, you've had ages to wash your hair,' Iain told her.

'Yeah, well,' she said cryptically.

'We're leaving in ten minutes,' Iain warned her, 'with or without you and your hair.'

'Have a nice time,' she said and Iain instantly regretted giving her a choice in the matter even if it had been a joke.

'*Ten* minutes,' he repeated. Honestly, how could he successfully steer a large international company and yet not be able to control one sixteen-year-old girl?

It was a four-hour journey from the MacNeice's Edinburgh home to the castle in the Highlands. Iain had studied the area carefully, noting the nearest town was Strathcorrie and remembering the little place from his childhood. He wondered what it would look like now. Places you hold dear from the past often had a habit of letting you down when revisited as an adult.

After an almighty argument over who was going to sit in the front passenger seat, and Iain soundly telling them that neither of them would until they acted like civil human beings, the girls settled down with a lapful of gadgets to keep them quiet, Chrissa in the front for the first leg of the journey.

Iain shook his head in wonder. In his time, he and his brother had had to make their own entertainment, playing 'I Spy' and making up silly sentences from the letters on car number plates. He doubted very much if Lexi or Chrissa would even look out of the window on the journey which was a crying shame because the landscape in this part of the Highlands really was something to behold.

Once they'd driven through the tiny town of Strathcorrie, the scenery seemed to explode, with mountains rising to great heights with snow-capped peaks. Silver-bright lochs greeted their gaze, the bruise-coloured clouds above reflected perfectly in their glassy stillness.

'Do you think it's going to snow, Daddy?' Chrissa asked. She was sitting on the back seat now, having swapped with Lexi after a stop at a service station.

'I hope not,' he said. 'At least not until we get to the castle.'

'I hope it snows. I want to build the world's biggest snowman!'

'I hate snow,' Lexi said. 'I like sunshine at Christmas.'

'That's the weirdest thing for a Scottish lass to say,' Iain said.

'I didn't choose to be born in Scotland,' Lexi said.

'Where would you have been born if you'd had the choice?' he asked her.

'California,' she said.

'Of course,' he said. He gritted his teeth. He was sick and tired of hearing about California these days.

It was several miles later when Iain decided to pull over on the side of a narrow road before it rose high up into the lowering clouds.

'We should have seen the turn-off by now,' he said. 'Have you got the directions?'

Lexi fumbled in the glove box and pulled out the printed email Iain had been sent and handed it to her father.

'Strathcorrie ... loch ... row of pines.' He looked out of the back window. 'Did either of you see a boulder with an arrow on it? Chrissa?'

'No,' Chrissa said. She'd gone back to her tablet and probably wouldn't have noticed if the Loch Ness monster had crossed the road in front of the car.

'Lexi?'

'Nope.'

'I think we must have missed it,' he said, turning the car around and driving back slowly. A minute later and there was the boulder. Sitting to the right of the road with a large white arrow painted onto it and the words: *Caldoon Castle.*

'Ah, good. Here's the turn off,' he said, slowing the car down to take an unmetalled road.

'This feels like the beginning of a horror film,' Lexi said.

'It is a little bit spooky,' Iain said.

'I don't like spooky,' Chrissa said, putting her tablet away and leaning forward between the front seats as they drove down the driveway.

'How far is it to the castle?' Lexi said. 'I thought we'd have seen it by now.'

'It's another two miles,' Iain said.

'Two miles?' Lexi said. 'They've got a two-mile driveway?'

'Sure looks like it,' he said with a grin.

'But there's nothing out here,' she said, staring into the vast open wilderness as the wind whipped over the rough grassland and through the trees.

'Not everyone lives in a big city,' he said.

'Anyone who lives out here must be mad,' Lexi said.

They drove on, passing a herd of Highland cattle, their long chestnut fur blowing in the wind and their enormous curved horns making them look prehistoric in the middle of the timeless landscape.

Iain opened his window and inhaled. 'Fresh air!' he said.

'Awww, Dad!' Lexi groaned. 'It's freezing!'

'Get a lungful of that,' he said. 'The air doesn't smell like that in Edinburgh, does it?'

'No, thank God,' Lexi said.

'What do you think of it, Chrissa?'

'It smells all clean,' she said.

'It does, doesn't it?'

'And cold,' she added and Iain nodded, closing the window quickly.

The driveway dipped down and rose up again, bending sharply to the right and that's when they got their first glimpse of Caldoon Castle with its high walls, romantic turrets and imposing castellations.

'Wow! Chrissa said, her bright eyes wide in wonder. 'It's like a fairytale.'

Iain beamed at his daughter's praise.

'It looks bloody freezing to me,' Lexi said.

'Language!' Iain said.

'Well, it does,' she said.

'Why do you always have to think of the negative, Lexi?' he asked.

'Because I'm a realist,' she said.

'Oh, really?' he said, wondering when his daughter had become so mature.

'I should be flying across the Atlantic to LA by now, on my way to Mum's swimming pool.'

'Yeah, well you're not,' Iain told her pragmatically.

'But I should be,' Lexi muttered, just loud enough that her father would hear her. 'Whoever heard of holidaying in Scotland, anyway?'

'I'll have you know, when I was your age–'

'What – back in the Dark Ages?'

'When I was your age,' Iain went on undeterred, 'we spent all our holidays in Scotland.'

'God, how boring!'

'Don't blaspheme,' he said

'Why not? We're not religious,' she said.

'It doesn't sound nice coming from a young lady.'

Lexi tutted.

'Anyway,' Iain continued, 'we spent every holiday in Scotland, climbing mountains, wading into rivers and swimming in lochs.'

'You're not expecting us to swim in a loch, are you?' Lexi said in horror.

'No, of course not,' Iain said with a laugh. 'We'll come back in the summer and do that.'

'Not likely,' Lexi said.

'I like Scotland,' Chrissa said.

'I'm very glad to hear it,' Iain told her.

'I like that you don't have to get on a plane and have your ears hurt to get here.'

'Let me tell you both something,' Iain said. 'It'll save you years of wasted time and no end of wasted money: travelling is highly overrated. There seems to be such a pressure on everyone to fly to the ends of the earth to experience something that they allegedly can't get at home, but that's just a myth. I don't think there's a more beautiful country than Scotland. England's not bad either, but it isn't Scotland. So you don't need to go back-packing in India and get Delhi Belly, or go traipsing through some rainforest and get bitten to death by insects the size of your hands.'

'No, you can get bitten to death right here in Scotland by the midges,' Lexi said.

Iain sighed and shook his head. Why was it so impossible to hold a cheerful conversation with his elder daughter?

'I never asked to come here,' she said and something inside Iain snapped and he hit the brakes.

'DAD!' Lexi screamed.

Iain turned the engine off, unfastened his seatbelt and turned sideways to glare at her.

'That's it, Alexandra!' he shouted.

'What?' she shouted back but he could tell that she was scared. Her beautiful dark eyes were twice their normal size and she'd turned quite pale. She knew she'd rattled him.

'I've really had enough of your constant complaints and your snidey little remarks.'

'What's *snidey* mean? Chrissa asked.

'I've been looking forward to this holiday for a long time. I can't remember the last time I had a proper holiday. I've worked hard so that I could take time off to be with you and Chrissa and I *don't* want to spend that time listening to your disgruntled remarks, okay?'

'What's *disgruntled*?' Chrissa asked.

'Is that clear?' Iain said.

'Yes,' Lexi said, her voice barely above a whisper.

'Pardon?'

'I said yes!' she said again.

'Good!' Iain said, a little calmer now as he did his seatbelt back up and started the engine.

'Daddy?' Chrissa said from the back seat.

'What is it?'

'Look!' Chrissa pointed to something at the top of the castle. It was an enormous flag flying in the fading light. 'It's got writing on it.'

'What does it say?' Iain asked, squinting up at the battlements.

'It says "Merry Christmas"!' Chrissa said with glee.

Iain grinned, thinking that was a nice touch. 'Come on, let's get inside before it's dark.'

He parked alongside an ancient Land Rover in the ample drive outside the castle and all three of them got out of the car. Iain opened the boot and they each took charge of their own cases before walking towards the entrance.

A huge metal bell hung to the side of perhaps the largest front door Iain had ever seen.

'Want to ring it, Lexi?' Iain asked his daughter.

'Nah,' she said and then caught her father's warning look. 'Okay.' She put her case down and gave the bell a good tug.

'Fun, eh?' he said.

'Yeah,' she said with a fake smile. 'I've never had so much fun in my life.'

They waited for a few moments.

'Do you think they heard us?' Chrissa asked.

'I don't know,' Iain said. 'It's a pretty vast place, isn't it?'

'Shall I ring it this time?' Chrissa said and her hand was just reaching up to sound the bell when the great wooden door was opened and a woman in her late-thirties greeted them.

'Mr MacNeice?' she said.

'Yes,' he said.

'Welcome to Caldoon Castle. Please come in. I'm Catriona Fraser.' She shook his hand and ushered them all into an enormous entrance hall which seemed to be made entirely out of wood with its shiny floorboards, wood panelled walls and great wooden staircase.

'Please call me Iain,' he said, 'and these are my daughters, Alexandra and—'

'It's Lexi,' Lexi said.

'And Chrissa,' Iain finished.

'Lovely to meet you, girls. Did you have a good journey from Edinburgh?'

'Not too bad. It was a bit icy on the road from Strathcorrie but, other than that, it was pretty trouble free,' he told her, taking in the amazing red hair which his hostess wore loose to her shoulders and her creamy complexion and bright hazel eyes.

It was then that the largest, hairiest dog in Scotland bounded across the hallway barking, causing Lexi and Chrissa to scream.

'Oh, don't be afraid!' Catriona cried. 'It's just Bagpipe. It's his way of welcoming you. *Quiet*, Baggy!'

Bagpipe stopped barking and walked slowly forward to sniff the new arrivals before slinking back off.

'Blimey,' Iain said, 'I don't think I've ever seen a bigger dog in my life. Is it an Irish wolfhound?'

'It's a Scottish deerhound,' Catriona said, 'and he might be big, but he's an absolute lamb.'

'He's incredible,' Iain said.

'They're one of the oldest breeds,' she told him and his daughters, 'and there's always been one at Caldoon Castle. There's probably an old legend stating that the castle will fall into ruin if there isn't one living here.'

'Daddy – look!' Chrissa said, tugging his arm and pointing to a huge suit of armour standing in the shadows. Its metal was a dull silver and it wasn't in great condition but it was still pretty impressive.

'We should get one of those for our hallway,' Iain said.

Chrissa giggled. 'It wouldn't fit!'

'We liked your flag too,' Iain said.

'Oh, good,' Catriona said. 'We normally fly the Fraser coat of arms but we like to celebrate special occasions too.' She smiled. 'Now, before we head upstairs, I'll just show you the rooms that are set aside for you on the ground floor.' They crossed the hallway together and Catriona opened a door into a beautiful living room with two enormous Knole sofas heaped with cushions and a fireplace in which a roaring fire licked its way up the chimney.

'I think I'm going to like it here,' Iain said with an appreciative smile.

'You've also got the dining room next door where meals are served and there's the billiards room just off that. There's also a little kitchen you're welcome to use but I'll be taking care of your meals. Now the Great Hall is where you'll be having your Christmas dinner but it isn't quite ready yet so I hope you don't mind if I don't show that to you until later. There's just a few finishing touches to organise.'

Iain nodded. 'Sounds exciting,' he said.

'Now, I'll show you to your rooms. I expect you'd like to rest after your journey.'

'Can we look around the rest of the castle?' Chrissa asked.

'Not just yet, Chrissa,' Iain said.

'But I want to see the tower with the little windows,' she said.

'I'll tell you what,' Catriona said, 'we can go via the old part of the castle. It's a wee bit longer but I think you'll like it. Leave your bags in the hall and I'll get them up to your rooms later, okay?'

Chrissa nodded in enthusiasm and the journey began.

CHAPTER 4

They didn't go up the impressive wooden staircase in front of them but took a little door half-hidden in the wood panelling. It led through a sparse hallway which felt cold and slightly damp and then turned left.

'Now, the steps are quite steep here,' Catriona warned as she opened a door to her right. 'Will you be okay with that?'

'I'm sure we will,' Iain said, curious as to what lay ahead of them. He could feel the young boy inside him awakening after a very long sleep and realised that he hadn't felt so excited since his thirteenth birthday when he had gone camping in the Cairngorms with his father. Excitement for him today meant closing deals, making money, selling concepts. All that was a good feeling, of course, but it wasn't excitement at a cellular level, he thought. Somewhere, in the mix and muddle of growing up, he'd lost the ability to seek out the thrill that came from something as basic as exploring an ancient castle and that was a great shame.

Catriona switched the light on and led the way up a spiral staircase, the narrow stone steps worn away in the middle by generations of feet. The walls were whitewashed and tiny windows greeted them at intervals as they climbed, only it was dark outside now and impossible to see the countryside that surrounded them.

'Keep hold of the rope handrail,' she told them.

'You all right, girls?' Iain asked, pausing for a moment.

'It's fun!' Chrissa said.

'Lexi?'

'Still here,' she said from the back.

'This is the oldest part of the castle,' Catriona said as she continued upwards. 'The tower is fifteenth-century.'

They continued climbing, endlessly spiralling higher before coming to a door and a landing.

'Does it go any higher?' Iain asked. He'd noticed the wooden door preventing them from climbing any further.

Catriona nodded. 'But it's not safe,' she said. 'At least not for visitors. We keep it locked and the key is kept safely out of harm's way. I still climb up there to change the flag but it's a bit dicey.'

'That doesn't sound advisable,' Iain said, suddenly anxious for the safety of his hostess to whom he'd taken an immediate shine.

'I'm used to it,' she said, shrugging her shoulders. 'I know where to step and where not to step. Right, follow me.'

They walked along another hallway and then took a staircase down a couple of floors.

'I'm going to get lost here!' Chrissa said.

'No you're not,' Iain said, 'because you're not to go wandering off.' As soon as the words were out of his mouth, he suddenly realised how grown-up and – well – boring he sounded. Hadn't he just felt his own heartbeat accelerate at the simple pleasure of exploring a castle? And was he seriously going to stop his own daughter from experiencing something as thrilling as that?

'What I mean,' he added, 'is that you're to make sure you let me know when you're going to do a bit of exploring, okay?' Well, that wasn't quite the free-spirited father he longed to be either but at least he was relaxing a little bit.

Chrissa nodded.

'How far is it to the nearest town?' Lexi asked.

'That would be Strathcorrie,' Catriona said.

'We drove through there on the way,' Iain said.

'That funny little place with the tartan shop?'

'A Touch of Tartan,' Catriona said.

'That's miles away!' Lexi said, her eyes filled with horror.

'A twenty-four mile round trip,' Catriona said. 'But don't worry – we've got everything we need to enjoy Christmas without leaving the castle.'

Lexi didn't look convinced.

They walked on through a carpeted hallway. This part of the castle felt distinctly warmer than the one they'd left behind and Iain noticed that there were paintings and photographs hanging on the walls and great silver sconces holding real candles.

Catriona halted at a door on the left. 'This is your room, Mr Mac–'

'Iain, please.'

'Oh, yes. Iain,' she said as she led them into the room. 'I hope you'll be very comfortable here.'

Iain took in the splendour of the large bedroom with its grand four-poster bed. The bed's ornately carved oak posts were as thick as tree trunks and the bedspread was richly embroidered in jewel-like reds and blues.

A tapestry in blues, greens and gold hung on the main wall. It depicted a stag in a mountain forest and Iain imagined that he'd be able to see such a scene if he only looked out of one of the castle windows as soon as it was light.

A mountain of tartan rugs was neatly folded on a dark wooden chest and there was a little table on which sat a kettle, a tray and an assortment of tea and biscuits including his favourite Highland shortbread.

'This is beautiful,' he said, turning to his hostess.

'Wow!' Chrissa said. 'It's really cool, Dad.'

Iain smiled down at Chrissa and then looked at Lexi. For once in her life, she wasn't wearing an entrenched frown.

'I don't know what to say,' Iain told Catriona. 'Are all the rooms like this?'

'Er, no,' Catriona said. 'It would be too expensive to keep all the rooms running, I'm afraid.'

'That seems a shame,' Iain said.

'Ah, it's just the way it is,' she said. 'The girls' rooms are along the corridor. Come with me.'

They left the master bedroom, following Catriona along the hallway and passing a series of small oil paintings of Highland landscapes.

'I thought Chrissa might like this room,' Catriona said, opening the door into a pretty room lined with floral wallpaper in pink and white which had a single bed heaped with cushions.

'Do you like it, sweetheart?' Iain asked and Chrissa nodded, her smile stretched across the whole of her face.

'Thank you!'

'You're welcome,' Catriona said. 'You're next door, Lexi.'

They all went to see what lay in store for her.

The room wasn't as luxurious as the master bedroom, nor was it as girly as the bedroom Chrissa had, but it had a quiet elegance about it with its muted autumnal colours and beautiful Victorian metal bed.

'Lexi?' Iain prompted. 'Do you like it?'

'It's okay, I suppose,' she said.

'That's high praise,' Iain quickly told Catriona.

'But I'd rather be in LA,' Lexi added.

'LA?' Catriona said, obviously puzzled.

Iain sighed. 'Lexi, for the last time, *this* is where we're spending Christmas so get used to it.'

She threw him an unhappy look and then walked into her room and flopped down onto the bed.

'You've got your own ensuite and a wonderful view of the loch during the day from this window.'

'So,' Iain said, clearing his throat, 'where are you if we need to find you?'

'We're in the east wing,' Catriona said. 'Down the hallway and turn left.'

He nodded. 'Thank you.'

'I'll leave you to settle in,' she said, 'but give me a shout if you need anything. Your bags will be with you shortly.'

Chrissa ran back into her room and Iain was left alone with Catriona for a moment.

'Is – erm – Lexi okay?' she asked him gently in a whisper.

Iain sighed. 'She's not happy about being here,' he said, 'and she's making life pretty miserable letting us know that.'

'Oh, dear,' Catriona said. 'How old is she?'

'Sixteen.'

'My Fee is fifteen. It's a tricky age, isn't it? So much going on in those teenage heads and we ancient adults can't begin to remember what it was like – at least that's what they think.'

'Everything I say and do seems to be the wrong thing.'

Catriona nodded. 'Maybe she'll get along with Fee.'

'It might be good to introduce them to each other,' he said.

'Leave that with me,' Catriona said and Iain immediately felt like a great weight had been lifted from him.

Catriona left the MacNeices to make themselves comfortable and returned downstairs to find Brody. He was in the kitchen and was in the process of helping himself to a cookie from the tin when she walked in.

'Oh no you don't!' she said, wagging a warning finger at him. 'Not until you've helped me take up the MacNeice's luggage.

'They're here then?' Fee said as she entered the kitchen. 'I saw their posh car.'

'Is it posh?'

'Looks brand new to me.'

'Anything looks brand new compared to our ancient Land Rover,' Catriona said.

'So, what are they like?' Fee asked.

'Why don't you find out by grabbing a suitcase and helping me and Brody out?'

Fee rolled her eyes. 'I walked right into that one, didn't I?'

'You certainly did!' Catriona said. 'Stay there, Baggy.'

Leaving the deerhound in his enormous basket by the range, the three of them left the kitchen and walked through to the hallway where the MacNeice's cases were.

'One each, okay?' Catriona said.

'I was hoping they would get lost on the moors and never find us,' Fee said as she grabbed one of the cases.

'That's not a very kind thing to say at Christmas. Or at any other time of the year for that matter,' Catriona said.

'Well, I don't feel very kind with a bunch of strangers in our house.'

'We've had this conversation before, Fee. This house is much too large *not* to share. If I showed you the heating bill alone—'

'I know, Mum,' she said with a sigh, 'but I don't have to *like* the fact that we're sharing at Christmas, do I?'

'I'd like you to make an effort to be nice to them,' Catriona said. 'Besides, I think you'll get on with Lexi. She's sixteen.'

'Just because we're nearly the same age, it doesn't mean we're going to get on.'

'I know,' Catriona said tolerantly, 'but you can at least try, can't you?'

'If you really want me to,' Fiona said with a pout.

'I do.'

The three of them trundled upstairs with the luggage and knocked on Iain's door first.

'Settling in okay?' Catriona asked when he opened it.

'Yes, thank you,' he said, taking his suitcase. 'I love the brown water in the bathroom.'

'It's because of the peat on the moors,' Catriona said. 'Makes the water wonderfully soft although it does scare the occasional guest.'

'I'd forgotten about that,' he said.

Catriona cocked her head to one side. 'Forgotten?'

'I grew up round here.'

'Did you?'

He nodded. 'The other side of Strathcorrie. A little village called North Lonan.'

'I know it!'

'Do you?'

'It's a lovely little spot,' she said.

'I haven't been back this way for years,' he said.

'So why now?' she asked and then caught herself. 'Sorry. Too nosy.'

'No, no,' he said. 'It's just–' he paused. 'It's time.'

She nodded and then remembered that her children hadn't yet been introduced to him. 'Fee, Brody – come and meet Mr MacNeice.'

The two of them walked into the room from the hallway.

'Pleased to meet you,' he said with a nod and a smile. 'Thank you for letting us stay in your beautiful home.'

Fee cleared her throat.

'You have something to say, Fee?' Catriona asked.

Fee shot her mother a look but then turned back to Mr MacNeice. 'We hope you enjoy your stay,' she said and Catriona sighed with relief.

'Right, let's get these cases to your daughters,' Catriona said and led Fee and Brody out of the room.

Chrissa greeted them with a big bright smile and a cheery hello but, unsurprisingly, Lexi didn't.

'We've got your suitcase, Lexi,' Catriona said after politely knocking on the door. 'Where shall I put it?'

Lexi was sprawled out on the bed, her arm across her face and Catriona couldn't help wondering if she'd been crying as her skin looked slightly flushed.

'Anywhere,' she mumbled.

'I'd like to introduce you to Fee and Brody,' Catriona continued undaunted.

Lexi got up from the bed, rubbing her eyes. 'Hi,' she said in a small voice and, for all her attitude and grouchiness, Catriona could see just how young and vulnerable she was and felt an instant urge to give her a cuddle.

'Hi,' Fee said from the doorway. The two teens eyed each other warily and then something extraordinary happened. 'I like your scarf.'

Catriona looked at her daughter and then looked at Lexi. She hadn't noticed the little chiffon scarf the teenager was wearing but she looked at it now and noticed that it was, indeed, very pretty.

'My mum sent it to me. It's from America. I've got more in my case if you'd like to see.'

'Sure,' Fee said.

Brody nudged his mum's arm. 'Can I go and play with Bagpipe?' he asked.

'Yes,' Catriona said, 'let's leave these two to it, shall we?'

As they passed Iain's room on the way back, Catriona knocked and entered. He was hanging shirts up in the dark wooden wardrobe but stopped and greeted her with a smile.

'I thought you'd like to know that our two teenagers have hit it off,' she said.

'Really? Already?'

Catriona nodded.

'Wow,' he said. 'If that's the case, I'm coming here *every* Christmas!'

Catriona left the room and a part of her couldn't help wishing that he was in earnest about spending every Christmas at the castle and she wasn't just thinking about her bank balance.

CHAPTER 5

It felt strange having a man in the castle again at Christmas, Catriona couldn't help thinking as she cleared her family's things away the next morning. The three Frasers had already taken Bagpipe out for a good long walk around the loch and he was snoring sonorously in his basket now.

She wondered if Iain MacNeice liked to walk. His shoulders had looked all hunched and stiff when he'd arrived and he looked as if he could do with a good stride around the loch and up over the moors. But it wasn't her place to interfere with her guests.

In the past, many of her guests hadn't left the comfort of their rooms, choosing to stay in the relative warmth with a good book or an electronic gadget. That seemed such a waste to Catriona who wanted to shake them out of their stupor and show them the beauty of the world around them for, even on the bleakest of days, there was always something of wonder to see at Caldoon. Take that very day. Hadn't the pale silvery morning been magical? Freezing, but magical. And everybody needed a bit of magic in their lives, didn't they?

When she'd first moved in as Andrew's wife, the two of them had spent hours walking on the estate together. Ostensibly, it had been to introduce her to life at Caldoon and how the place was run but, more often than not, it was just an excuse for the two of them to pack up a hamper and spend time together. Then Fiona had been born and life had changed forever. Brody followed a few years later and picnics by the loch – although still romantic – were never quite the same again.

A light knock on the kitchen door brought Catriona back to the present.

'Good morning,' Iain said, popping his head round the door. 'We didn't see you after dinner last night and I wanted to thank you for a lovely meal. Your dining room's really amazing'

'I hoped you'd like it. It was pretty misty first thing and I was anxious that you wouldn't get the view down to the loch from there.'

'It's a great view,' he said. 'I'd forgotten how beautiful it is up here.' He ran a hand through his hair. 'I seem to have forgotten to make time to just stand and look at views.'

Catriona caught a look in his eyes that was wistful and melancholic.

'Perhaps that's what's brought you here,' she told him, 'to give you the time to stand and look around you.'

'Maybe,' he said. 'I hope so. But it's more about spending quality time with my girls. I don't see them enough and it kills me.' He swallowed hard and looked down at the floor as if embarrassed that he'd said too much.

'Well, there'll be plenty of time to remedy that at Caldoon. There's plenty of time here. Time and space.'

He looked up again and smiled at her. 'Good to know,' he said and she suddenly felt shy at looking at him – almost as if she was intruding. So she brought the subject round to something safe.

'Are you ready for the works?' she asked.

'I beg your pardon?'

'Breakfast!'

'Oh, yes! Well, no. Actually, *I* am,' he said, 'but Chrissa only wants scrambled eggs.'

'And Lexi?' Catriona asked.

He shook his head. 'She's been stirring the same bit of porridge around for the last ten minutes.'

'Oh, dear,' she said. 'Do you think she'd like a hot chocolate?'

'That's very kind of you. She might just go for that.'

'It's a rare young lady who doesn't enjoy a hot chocolate.'

He nodded and she watched as he left the kitchen and she felt her heart ache for this sweet man who didn't have enough time to spend with his daughters and then wasn't quite sure what to do with them when he did have the time.

Chrissa had spread some of her coloured pens out on the breakfast table and was working on an intricate floral design in one of her colouring-in books and Lexi was attempting to use her mobile phone.

'I can't get a signal,' she complained. 'I've tried all over the place.'

'Try the hallway,' Iain said. 'By the window.' He'd managed to get a signal there earlier that morning, checking in to see if there had been any last minute panics at his company but all had been quiet.

Lexi was on her feet and out of the room in a second.

'Come back in a minute. Catriona's got something for you,' Iain called after her. He looked across the table towards Chrissa who was thoroughly absorbed in her work with a purple pen.

'What are you colouring?' he asked, moving forward and leaning over her shoulder.

'A flower,' he said.

'You're a flower,' he said, bending to kiss her head. She giggled and his heart melted. She was the sweetest girl in the world, wasn't she? Lexi had been just like her only a few years ago, he thought, remembering back to the times when they'd been able to laugh together. So what had happened to make her so spiky and resentful? Was it just the fact that she was a teenager or did she blame him for the breakdown of his marriage to Dawn?

He sighed as he moved towards the large mullioned window which looked out towards the loch. The light was an eerie sepia colour and the landscape of open moors and mountains before him looked like an old photograph. He hadn't really realised until now just how much he'd missed the Highlands. His own childhood holidays when they'd camped and trekked through the forests and hiked up the mountains and swam in the lochs had been so much fun. Why hadn't he thought to bring the girls here before?

The last few years had been so stressful with the separation and he hadn't given holidays much thought at all. He'd been quite relieved when Dawn had taken the pressure off him and had the girls to stay with her in California. She'd been brought up there, had never really got used to the Scottish climate and had probably been mightily relieved to return there, walking out on twenty-two years of marriage without so much as a backwards glance.

He knew what was to blame for the breakdown of his marriage, of course: him. Him and his work. But how could he have changed that? When he'd left the advertising firm where he'd worked for over a decade, he'd had to build his own company from the ground up and the hours he'd put into the business had been crippling, especially the last few years. Dawn hadn't been happy. He'd been spending less time with his family and had once even made them all return early from a family holiday so he could attend to business.

She'd liked the money, though, he thought with a wry grin: the money that had allowed them to move to the beautiful Georgian apartment in Edinburgh. She'd liked the clothes she'd been able to buy for herself and the girls, and she'd liked having help around the home. All those things cost money and he'd been good at providing it. But what was the real cost? Had he lost the very thing he'd been working so hard for?

'Here we are,' Catriona said, entering the room with a heaped tray of food and breaking the negative spiral of his thoughts.

'That looks fantastic,' he said, watching as she put a very full plate of eggs, bacon and the rest of the works on the table. She then placed Chrissa's plate of buttery toast and scrambled eggs next to her after helping her to clear her pens away.

'Lexi?' Catriona said.

'Ah, yes, let me find her,' Iain said, leaving the room in search of her. He found her sitting on the staircase looking miserable, her phone in her hand.

'I couldn't get a signal,' she said.

'Never mind,' he said, 'we'll try and find somewhere later, okay? Maybe take a drive out.'

She seemed to cheer up at this and followed him back into the dining room.

'I've made you a hot chocolate,' Catriona told her.

Lexi sat down next to her sister. 'Thank you,' she said.

'Is there anything else I can get you?' Catriona asked, tucking a strand of her long red hair behind her ear. It really was the most extraordinary colour, Iain couldn't help thinking, as warm and vibrant as a blazing fire in the heart of winter.

'Girls?' Iain said.

'No, thank you,' Chrissa and Lexi said together.

'Looks like we're all good, thank you,' Iain said with a smile before diving into his breakfast. 'So, what do you two want to do today?' he asked his daughters as Catriona left the room.

Chrissa gave a little shrug as she ate her eggs and toast.

'Lex?'

She looked up from her hot chocolate. 'Do we have to do anything?'

'We've come all this way,' he said.

'But what's there to do in the middle of winter in the Highlands?' she asked.

'We could go for a walk around the loch,' he suggested.

'Really?'

'It's beautiful out there whatever the weather's doing. We could wrap up warm. It would be fun.'

'You have a *really* weird sense of fun, Dad,' she said.

Catriona allowed the MacNeices plenty of time to finish breakfast before she and Fee cleared the table together.

'How did you get on with Lexi yesterday?' she asked her daughter.

'She's cool,' Fee said. 'She has so many clothes and they're all really nice. And her dad buys her really expensive things like designer sunglasses and watches and stuff.'

'Don't keep saying *stuff*,' Catriona said. 'Be more specific.'

'Aw, Mum – we're on holiday now and you promised to stop being a teacher.'

'I'm not being a teacher; I'm being your mother.'

Fee groaned. 'All right then – *things*. Her dad buys her all these *things*!'

'And?'

'What?'

'What's your point?' Catriona asked her daughter.

'There's no point. I'm just saying.'

Catriona took a deep breath, realising that her insecurities had got the better of her because she knew that she couldn't buy her children lots of designer stuff. *Things*. They shopped in the sales. They bought second-hand. They wore clothes until they had more holes than material. That was their life. Not for them was shopping on Princes Street buying ridiculously expensive labels.

'Okay,' she said to her daughter, 'but I don't think those things make her happy.'

Fee looked at her mum. 'What do you mean?'

'I mean, I've never seen a more unhappy young woman in my life, have you?'

'She is rather glum,' Fee said.

'*Things* or *stuff* don't make you happy,' Catriona told her daughter.

'What does, then?'

'Family, friends, home, a job you love,' Catriona said.

Brody came into the dining room with his pet rat, Hank, on his shoulder. 'What are we talking about?' he asked.

'What makes us happy,' Catriona said.

'Hank makes me happy,' he said, tickling the toffee-coloured rat.

'He makes my skin crawl!' Fee said, giving one of her theatrical shudders.

'What else makes you happy, Brody?' Catriona asked as they took the dishes through to the kitchen.

'Erm, my computer,' he said, 'my phone.'

'See, Mum,' Fee said, 'that's stuff.'

'But what is he using his stuff for? To talk to friends, right?'

'I guess,' Brody said. 'Why?'

'Mum's trying to persuade me that expensive stuff doesn't make you happy.'

'Is this her way of saying that our Christmas presents are all home-made?' he asked.

'No!' Catriona said, plonking the plates in the sink and placing her hands on her hips. 'I'm just trying to say that there are other things in life which matter more. Like seeing a beautiful sunset or watching an eagle high above the mountain.'

'As long as you don't try and fob those things off on us as Christmas presents,' Fee said.

Catriona threw the dishcloth in the sink. She knew when to give up in defeat.

The walk around the loch wasn't a complete success, Iain had to admit. It was much further than it looked from the windows of the castle and the December wind pummelled and pounded them, causing earache, watering eyes and – even worse – tatty hair. By the time they got back to the castle Lexi was in a foul mood, pulling her beanie from her head and cursing her father for her knotted locks.

'Just look!' she cried.

'Don't worry, darling,' he said. 'Nobody's going to see you.' As soon as the words were out and he saw his daughter's face, he knew it had been the wrong thing to say.

'You just don't care, do you?' she said, before stomping up the stairs to her bedroom.

'What does she think I don't care about?' he asked Chrissa whose tattered locks didn't seem to be causing her quite as much angst.

'Her,' she said.

'But why would she think that?' he asked. 'Chrissa? Tell me. What's she been saying?'

'Nothing,' Chrissa said. 'She doesn't talk to me. She says I'm too young.' Her whole body seemed to sink with this statement. 'Why am I so much younger than she is, Daddy?'

Iain wrapped her up in a warm embrace. 'It's just the way things worked out,' he said. 'We wanted you much, *much* sooner, but you weren't ready to make an appearance.'

'And Lexi *was* ready to make an appearance?'

'More than ready,' Iain said, thinking of the day when Dawn had announced she was pregnant. They'd been living in the tiniest of flats on the outskirts of Edinburgh and panic had almost got the better of them. But they'd ridden it out and had fallen in love with their little baby girl as soon as she'd arrived. 'Perhaps I should talk to her.'

Chrissa shook her head as if she was trying to dislodge a wasp from her ear.

'What?' he asked.

'Not when she's like that. She's mean when she's like that.'

'Oh, right,' he said.

'Everything okay?' Catriona asked as she came into the hallway, Bagpipe the deerhound following.

'Still trying to work that one out,' he said.

'Lexi?' Catriona said.

Iain nodded. 'We went for a walk around the loch and her hair got messed up and I'm afraid I made a comment that upset her.'

'Would you like me to talk to her?'

'No, no, no,' Iain said hurriedly. 'This isn't your problem.'

'It is if it's under my roof,' she said, her mouth curving up ever-so-slightly at the edges.

'I can't expect you to step in here,' he said.

'But I do have some experience with teenage girls,' Catriona said, 'and I really don't mind.'

Her kindness touched him deeply and he was so desperate to try and find out what was wrong with Lexi that he was utterly helpless to refuse her offer, and so he nodded and watched as she walked up the stairs with Bagpipe charging ahead.

CHAPTER 6

Catriona couldn't help feeling anxious as she reached Lexi's bedroom door which was resolutely closed to the outside world. She paused, gathering her thoughts. What exactly was she going to say to this beautiful, sad girl? She really wasn't sure. But she knew she had to do something. The mother in her had kicked in the moment she'd seen the lost girl standing in her hallway on arrival and she knew she had to reach out to her.

'You wait here, Baggy,' she said to the deerhound who looked up at her with his mournful chocolate-coloured eyes as she knocked lightly on the door.

'Lexi?' she called softly. 'It's Catriona.' She waited a moment and then opened the door which, thankfully, wasn't locked. The room looked dark and gloomy with the thick velvet curtains shut against the morning and Catriona instinctively walked over to draw them.

'Please don't,' Lexi said. She was resting on her bed with her arm across her face.

'Are you not feeling well?' Catriona said, suddenly anxious as she let the curtains fall back into place.

'I'm fine,' Lexi said.

Oh, how Catriona hated the word "fine". How often did people use it when it was quite clear that they *weren't* fine? That they were about as far removed from fine as it was possible to get? If she had her own way, the word "fine" would be locked away in the deepest dungeon along with "stuff".

'Dad sent you, didn't he?' Lexi said, sitting up and pushing her hair out of her face.

'He's worried about you.'

'He doesn't want to talk to me.'

'I think he wants to talk to you more than anything else in the world, Lexi.'

The girl's dark eyes held her own and there was a rawness of emotion in them that made Catriona want to reach out and hug her.

'Will you talk to him?' she asked her, daring to reach out and squeeze her hand.

'I don't think I can,' Lexi said in a little voice.

'What makes you think that?'

'Because he's never around.'

'He's around now,' Catriona said.

'But I feel like I don't know him,' Lexi said and it was the saddest statement that Catriona had ever heard.

'Well, that's why he's made this time for you now,' she said.

Lexi gave a little shrug of her shoulders. They were much too thin for Catriona's liking and she made a mental note to make sure Lexi was well fed for the duration of her stay.

'Just because we're all stuck here together, it doesn't mean I have to talk to him. *He* wanted to come here, but I didn't.'

'But he's making a real effort,' Catriona said, 'and you've got to try and meet him half-way.'

Lexi swung her legs off the bed and got up. Catriona watched as she walked towards the dressing-room table and picked up a photo in a frame she'd brought with her. She looked at it and her gaze instantly softened.

'Can I see?' Catriona asked and Lexi held the frame out towards her.

'It was at the house we lived in before we moved to the New Town. I was ten and Chrissa was two.'

The two girls in the photo were sitting on the floor beside a Christmas tree bedecked with multi-coloured baubles and lights. But it wasn't just them in the photo. A dark-haired woman was sitting between them, smiling up at the camera. She was wearing a claret-coloured dress and a necklace of glowing amber beads. She looked like a heroine from a Pre-Raphaelite painting and Catriona was instantly captivated.

'It's a beautiful photo,' she said, handing it back to Lexi who gazed into the photo as if she hoped she might melt into it. 'You miss her, don't you?'

Lexi nodded. 'They're separated and Mum's living in America. It's horrible,' she said with a sniff. 'Not America – that's really cool. But I hate not seeing her every day and I hate that she doesn't ring every week now. She did at first, but not anymore.'

'It must be difficult for your dad too,' Catriona said gently. 'Think about it. He must miss your mum just as much as you do.'

'I don't think so,' Lexi said. 'He's too busy to miss anyone.'

'How do you know that?'

'He just thinks about his work and he's always late home.'

'But that doesn't mean he's not missing you. He probably wants to be home with you but can't be.'

'Why are you defending Dad like this? You don't know him.' The look of anger on Lexi's face instantly aged her by a decade.

'I'm trying to understand him, that's all. Like I'm trying to understand you now.'

'You're an adult – you're going to side with him,' Lexi said, reminding Catriona just how young and insecure this girl was.

'That's not a very fair assumption,' she said. 'Your dad might think I'll side with you because we're both female but that doesn't make it true, does it?'

Lexi looked lost. 'I don't know,' she said and she flopped down on the bed again, her shoulders sagging. 'Why is everything so complicated?'

'That's the way of the world,' Catriona said. 'We think we've got it all worked out and that our place in it is safe and secure and can't be shaken but that's the precise moment when it can. It happens to everyone, you know?'

Lexi turned her pale face to look at her. 'Has it happened to you?'

Catriona nodded and took a deep, steadying breath as she sat down on the bed. 'It has. My husband died two years ago.' As the words were spoken, she could feel her hands beginning to shake. She still found it so hard to talk about.

'Oh, no,' Lexi said.

'That's one of the reasons it's so hard for me to see you and your father so distant with each other. You know, Lexi, the bond between a father and a daughter is so special and I know Fee would give anything to have her father back.'

'What happened to him?' Lexi dared to ask.

'He had cancer,' Catriona said, and she saw tears rising in Lexi's eyes. 'Now, I'm not telling you this to make you sad or to make you feel sorry for us all. We're coping. It's not easy and the time around Christmas is always especially difficult. Andrew loved Christmas and we always did something special and silly. But I think you should know that life isn't perfect and that we all have to go through something that's going to rattle us, whether that's a difficult decision we have to make or a divorce or a death. It's all part of life and we have to get through it as best as we can.'

They sat in silence together on the edge of the bed, a blast of hail pattering on the window, making the bedroom feel even cosier with its curtains drawn against the inhospitable day. Catriona got up and switched the bedside lamp on and the room was bathed in its warm glow.

'Light is very important,' she said. 'You mustn't allow yourself to sit in the darkness for too long.'

Lexi looked up at her as if understanding.

There was then a strange whining from the hallway and the bedroom door was pushed open.

'Why's your dog doing that?' Lexi asked, turning to see Bagpipe's face appearing in the doorway.

'He knows when somebody's upset and he joins in.'

Lexi was on her feet, walking across the room with the speed of somebody on a mission.

'Don't cry,' she told the dog, bending so that she could wrap her arms around his great hairy neck. 'I'm not crying anymore.'

Catriona found Iain in the living room which had been given to his family for their exclusive use during their stay. He'd lit the fire and was sitting nursing a cup of strong-looking tea.

'How is she?' he asked as soon as Catriona walked into the room.

'Where's Chrissa?' she asked.

'In her room.'

Catriona nodded and sat down on the sofa opposite him and Bagpipe lay on the floor by her feet.

'She's upset,' she told him.

'She's been nothing *but* upset for the last three years,' he said. 'Upset and angry and resentful. I don't know what to do or say. Everything I try seems to be shot down by her. God, I'm doing a bad job!' His hair had flopped over his face and his cheeks were blazing red in frustration. Or maybe it was his proximity to the fire, Catriona thought. She couldn't be sure.

'You're not doing a bad job,' she told him.

'How can you say that? I'm not even coping on a *basic* level because I can't communicate with her.'

'She needs you to be patient with her,' Catriona said gently. 'She's almost a woman now and she's hasn't got the person she was closest to in the whole world near her. It's obvious that she idolises her mother.'

'You can see that?'

'Oh, yes,' Catriona said. 'She showed me a photo of her. She was holding it as if it was the most precious thing in the world to her.'

'The Christmas photo? She brought it with her?' Iain ran a hand through his hair which didn't exactly straighten it out, only pushed it in a different direction. 'She really misses her, doesn't she?'

'Were they close?' Catriona asked.

'Dawn adored her girls. Spoilt them rotten too. They were her world. Well, until they stopped being her world.' Iain gazed into the flames of the fire and Catriona was just wondering what was going through his mind when he started up again. 'I think she'd been unhappy with me for some time. I know I didn't spend enough time with her and she's the kind of woman who needs to have somebody around her all the time. I was at work day and night and the girls were at school. I think she just got jaded and bored. I tried to talk to her so many times, but she'd made her mind up. I could feel this coldness settling between us for months before she finally left.'

'And the girls stayed with you?'

Iain nodded. 'Their school and friends – everything's in Edinburgh and Dawn didn't want to disrupt that. But there was more to it than that. She wanted some time to herself. It was as if she'd given all she had to her children and had simply run out.'

Catriona didn't want to pass judgement on a woman she'd never met but she couldn't understand how any mother could leave her children.

'I know what you're thinking. How could she leave her girls?'

'Well, I–'

'It's the question I simply can't answer,' Iain said. 'When she was settled in the States, she sent for the girls and they've had a few holidays over there, but they've been getting fewer and fewer as the years go by and she told me categorically that she didn't want them this Christmas. It wasn't a case of, "They can stay with you," but more a "Don't even think of sending them over here."'

'So what's changed?' Catriona dared to ask.

'Did Lexi tell you that Dawn has a partner?'

'No, she didn't.'

'I'm not sure how much the girls know about it, and I don't know how long Dawn's been seeing him, but it sounds serious and – well – she wanted to spend Christmas with his family in San Francisco. The bottom line was she didn't want the girls there. I have a feeling she wants to be Dawn again – the pre-marriage Dawn who was beautiful and adored everywhere she went and didn't come with a couple of kids attached to her.'

'But you said she adored her daughters,' Catriona said, still trying to work it all out.

'She did!' Iain said, his voice unnaturally high. 'She changed and I wasn't there to stop her or to question her. We were both leading separate lives and somehow managed to drift away from each other.'

One of the fat logs on the fire shifted and a flurry of sparks flew up the dark chimney.

'Listen,' he said, 'I don't mean to burden you with all this.'

'You're not,' she said. 'I like to listen. It's one of the joys of having guests – I get to see little glimpses of the world. Living here can be very isolating.' She gave a little grin and he smiled back. 'Now,' she said, getting up and chucking another log onto the fire, 'I'm going to start lunch.'

'Will you all join us, please?'

'For lunch?'

'Yes. I think Lexi would like that,' he said, 'and I certainly would.' He looked at her, anxiety in his eyes as he awaited her answer.

'We'd be delighted,' she said.

'I can't believe it's Christmas Eve tomorrow,' Iain said as he finished his homemade pork pie.

'It's about time,' Brody said. 'I've been waiting for it all year.'

'He's not kidding,' Catriona said as she cleared the plates. 'I think he was telling me last Boxing Day what he wanted for next Christmas.'

Brody grinned, obviously knowing she was right.

'Did we leave mince pies out at home for Father Christmas?' Chrissa asked her father.

'No, darling. There's no point because all your presents will be delivered here,' he said, thinking about the gifts he'd smuggled out into the boot of the car before they'd left Edinburgh.

'I don't put mince pies out for Father Christmas,' Brody said. 'I put them out for the ghosts.'

'Ghosts?' Lexi said, her eyes gleaming.

Chrissa's mouth dropped open in alarm. 'Are there ghosts?'

'No, no,' Catriona said quickly. 'The castle isn't haunted. Not really. It's just a story Brody puts about to get attention.'

'It is haunted,' he said. 'I've heard them heavy breathing in the night.'

'That's just Bagpipe snoring,' Fee said.

Everyone laughed. Except Chrissa whose fork had halted half-way to her mouth at the first mention of ghosts.

'Chrissa,' Catriona said, 'I promise you there are no ghosts at Caldoon.'

'I expect you get a lot of visitors who want to see a ghost, right?' Iain said.

'Castles and ghosts do seem to go hand-in-hand as far as guests are concerned. I've often thought we should make one up. Of course, there was that time Brody dressed up in a bed sheet and terrified that dear old lady from Swindon. She said she was never going to set foot in Scotland again.'

Brody grinned.

'I don't know why people want to stay in castles,' Lexi said. Her father gave her an immediate warning glare. 'They're so cold and cobwebby, aren't they?'

'You're cold in your room?' Catriona asked.

'No,' Lexi said.

'There are cobwebs, then?'

'Not in my room,' Lexi said. 'I just meant—'

'You meant to say what a wonderful experience it is to stay here,' Iain said. 'That's right, isn't it?'

'No, I didn't, Dad. I think I should be honest. You're always saying how important honesty is.'

'Yes, but—'

'And I didn't want to come here,' she went on.

'Lexi – there's being honest and then there's being plain rude,' Iain said, his voice raising slightly.

'And I very much doubt if Chrissa really wanted to come here too. It's just she's too sweet to say anything.'

'Lexi – stop this right now.'

'We wanted to go to Mum's,' Lexi said. 'Didn't we, Chrissa? We wanted to spend Christmas with Mum.'

'Yeah?' Iain said. 'Well, I've got news for you, Lexi. Your mum didn't want you there, okay?'

The dining room filled with a deafening silence as all eyes turned to Iain.

'Lexi – I shouldn't have said that. I didn't mean–'

But it was too late to retract the words now. They were out there and had done their damage.

'Lexi–' he cried as his daughter got up from the table and bolted from the room.

Chrissa sat perfectly still, her mouth gaping open as if letting a wild, silent cry free, and her eyes filled with tears.

'Chrissa – sweetheart,' Iain said, getting up from his chair and pulling his daughter out from hers so he could hug her to him. 'I didn't mean that. I don't know why I said it.'

Chrissa didn't speak but the crying wasn't long in coming.

'My darling – don't cry!' Iain said as he stroked her dark hair. 'I'm here. I'm here.' He looked up and caught Catriona's eye. 'I didn't handle that very well, did I?' he said to her.

She bit her lip, obviously unsure what to say.

'You're in a difficult position,' she told him diplomatically.

'I don't know what I was thinking. She just pushed my buttons.'

'Don't blame yourself,' Catriona said. 'Listen, I'll go and find Lexi, okay?'

'Shall we help, Mum?' Fee said, standing up from the table.

Brody was on his feet too so as not to miss out on a potential adventure.

'I'll look as well,' he said. 'I know all the best hiding places in the castle and I'll find her if she's in one of them.'

CHAPTER 7

It wasn't until half an hour later that the panic set in.

'Iain, we can't find her,' Catriona announced as she, Fee and Brody met back in the living room. 'She's not in her room or anywhere on that entire floor.'

'And I've searched in all the hiding places,' Brody said, 'even the cobwebby ones where girls don't normally go.'

'She's not in the billiards room or the Great Hall either,' Fee said.

Iain's face was ashen. He was sitting on one of the sofas by the fire, Chrissa cuddling in next to him. 'You don't think she could have gone outside, do you?'

They all looked out of the window at the brooding afternoon with its grim grey clouds threatening snow.

'None of us heard the front door, did we?' Catriona asked.

Everyone shook their heads.

'I'll check the kitchen,' Brody said, disappearing before his mother could stop him.

'No cookies, Brody!' she shouted after him before turning back to Iain. 'How's Chrissa?'

'She's a bit calmer now,' Iain said.

Chrissa looked up at the mention of her name. 'Where's Lexi?'

'We're trying to find her, darling,' Iain said.

'Mum!' Brody said as he ran back into the room.

'What is it?' Catriona asked.

'The key to the tower's gone.'

Catriona and Iain locked eyes, their fear apparent.

'She wouldn't have taken it, surely?' Catriona said. 'She wouldn't have known where to look for a start although it's not that hard to find.'

'She's very good at finding things she shouldn't,' Iain said as he sprang up from the sofa. 'Let's go.'

Brody led the way, crossing the hall and following the route which the MacNeices had taken when they'd first arrived at the castle.

'Would she really have gone up there?' Iain asked.

'We'll soon find out,' Catriona said.

'What if she's done something stupid?'

'Don't even go there, Iain,' she told him, her hand resting briefly on his arm as they reached the door to the spiral staircase.

'Fee,' Catriona said, 'I want you to stay here with Chrissa, okay? Actually, on second thoughts, go back to the living room where it's warmer.'

'But, Mum—'

'No buts.'

Fee tutted but took hold of Chrissa's hand and did what she was told whilst Catriona, Iain and Brody headed up the stairs, setting off at the kind of urgent pace which prohibits speech.

Catriona could only imagine what was going through Iain's mind as they climbed towards the tower and, although she'd told him to banish any negative thoughts, she couldn't help going to the worst case scenario herself. What if Lexi had done something stupid? What would they do? How would Iain cope? And would her own children be able to cope? It was too black a place to visit.

You have to keep calm, she told herself. *Nothing's happened. Everything's going to be okay.*

But, when they reached the wooden door and found it unlocked, she couldn't suppress a feeling of terror.

'She did take the key,' Brody said. 'I was right!'

'Brody,' Catriona said, turning to him and placing her hands on his shoulders, 'I need you to stay here.'

'I *knew* you were going to say that!' he said with a sigh.

'Then you'll know that's the right thing to do,' she said calmly. 'The roof's a dangerous place, especially when it's icy.'

'I know,' he said.

'I'm going up,' Iain said, looking agitated at having to wait a second longer than was necessary.

'No,' Catriona said, 'let me go first. I know the layout of the roof – all the danger spots.'

He nodded his assent and the two of them walked up the remaining steps until they reached another wooden door.

'Brace yourself,' Catriona told him. 'It can get pretty wild up here.'

She opened the door and the gust of wind that greeted them instantly stole their breaths.

And there Lexi was. Huddled up against a castellated wall, her knees pressed to her chest and her dark hair flying wildly around her and the flag whipping high above her.

'Lexi!' Iain cried out. She didn't look up. Had she heard him?

Catriona caught his arm as he instinctively made a move towards his daughter.

'Let me,' she said. Iain nodded, his face pale and anxious.

Catriona walked out slowly onto the roof, mindful of the fact that they were five storeys up and that it was both windy and icy: possibly the worst conditions to be up there.

'Lexi, love,' Catriona said as she reached her, placing a hand on her arm.

The teenager looked up, her dark eyes filled with fear and Catriona noted that she was sitting dangerously close to the part of the roof that was in desperate need of repair.

'Let's get you down from here,' Catriona said.

'I can't move,' Lexi cried.

'Yes you can!' Catriona shouted above a sudden gust of wind. 'Take my hand. You're going to be all right.'

Lexi fixed her eyes on Catriona and then placed her hand in hers.

'That's it. Nice and slowly. Keep a tight grip of me.'

Lexi was barely on her feet when she slipped on a patch of ice, crying out in fright.

'Lexi!' Iain cried, rushing out onto the roof towards his daughter.

'It's okay – I've got you,' Catriona said, placing her arm around her. 'Don't walk there!' she shouted to Iain just before he reached a particularly unsafe part of the roof.

With baby steps, the three of them made it back to the door, shutting it behind them.

'She's frozen,' Catriona told Iain. 'We need to warm her up.'

Brody came up the stairs towards them.

'Brody – go ahead of us and let Chrissa and Fee know Lexi's okay. Then boil us a kettle and make a cup of tea and a hot water bottle for Lexi and bring them up to her room.'

'I'm fine,' Lexi said, but her pale face and the fact that she was shaking told quite another story.

Catriona and Iain helped her down the steps, reaching the landing that led to stairs and on down the hallway her bedroom.

'Let's get you into bed, love,' Catriona said, taking Lexi's shoes off. Lexi was wearing a thin cotton tunic-style dress over leggings which had become damp from her time on the roof. Catriona turned to Iain. 'I'm going to get her undressed, okay? We need to make sure she's dry.'

He nodded and ran into the ensuite for a towel.

'Here,' he said a moment later, turning his back as Catriona got to work.

Catriona worked as quickly as she could, undressing and drying Lexi who didn't protest. She was shivering which was a good sign as it was nature's way of getting a person to warm themselves up.

After dressing Lexi in her nightie and bed socks, which Catriona found on a chair by the bed, she helped her into bed and Iain sat down beside her, cradling her in his arms.

'Lexi, darling,' he said and then he turned to Catriona. 'We need to blast some heat at her.'

She shook her head. 'No, no. She needs to warm up gently and slowly. That's the way.'

'You don't think she's got hypothermia, do you?'

'I think she was quite close to getting it,' Catriona said as calmly as she could, 'but we've got her in time.'

It was then that Brody and the girls arrived with the tea and hot water bottle and Chrissa ran into the room, leaping onto the bed.

'Careful, Chrissa!' Iain warned but she'd already snuggled in next to her sister.

'We need to get this warm drink inside you, Lexi,' Catriona said as she took the mug of tea from Fee. 'Can you sit up for me? That's it. Nice and slowly.'

They all watched as Lexi sipped her drink and Catriona slipped the hot water bottle into the bed.

'We'll give you some space, okay?' she told Iain and he nodded.

'Listen,' he said, grabbing Catriona's hand as she left the bedroom, 'I can't thank you enough.'

'You don't have to,' she said, giving his hand a light squeeze before walking away.

CHAPTER 8

Iain's heart was heavy and his mind racing as he thought about what had just happened. He looked at Lexi, who had put her mug of tea down and was wrapped warmly under the duvet with Chrissa snuggled up next to her, and something inside him seemed to burst and he squeezed her tightly to him.

'Daddy!' Chrissa cried, half in surprise and half in delight as he flung his arms around her too.

'Lexi, Lexi, Lexi!' he cried. 'What were you thinking?'

'I don't know,' she said, a sob in her voice as he squashed her to him. 'I just had to get away. I had to–'

'You scared us half to death!' he confessed.

'I'm sorry! I didn't mean to.'

'You mean the world to me, Lex. I don't know what I'd do without you and Chrissa.'

The three of them embraced one another, crying and clinging in equal measure for what seemed like an eternity.

Finally, Iain looked up, wiping his eyes with a tissue from his pocket. The room seemed horribly silent all of a sudden and he wasn't quite sure what to say or do. Nothing had ever prepared him for such a situation and he felt utterly lost and half-wished that Catriona would walk in with a cup of tea and her pretty little smile. But she didn't. He was on his own and so he took a deep breath. But he didn't have a chance to say anything because Lexi beat him to it.

'You were speaking the truth about Mum, weren't you?' she said, as he wiped the tears from her cheeks and tucked her hair behind her ears, which made her look so very young. 'She didn't want us with her, did she?'

Iain sighed. How could he possibly answer such a question? 'Lexi – listen to me,' he began.

'I think I've known it for a while,' Lexi interrupted.

'What?' he asked, shocked by her statement.

'The way she's been acting when we've been with her and the fact that she doesn't ring us as much now,' Lexi said. 'It's like she's a different person now.'

Iain nodded sadly. 'I'm so sorry to hear that, darling,' he said. 'I wish there was something I could say to make this all better but know this – your mother does love you. So, *so* much but it's in a different way now.'

Chrissa looked up at him and the expression on her face nearly slayed him.

'I miss her,' she said.

'I know you do,' he said, kissing the top of her head. 'But you'll always have me. I might not be much but I'm not going anywhere.'

'Oh, Daddy!' Lexi cried and the three of them hugged once more, their heads touching as the tears began again.

Down in the kitchen, Brody had helped himself to a cookie and Catriona hadn't reprimanded him because her son had earned it.

'Pass the tin,' she told him and her hand dived in.

'That was close,' Fee said, shaking her head when Catriona offered her a cookie.

'Toooooo damned close!' Brody said.

'Language!' Catriona said.

'Yeah, but the situation calls for it, Mom!'

She shook her head in despair. She really was going to have to ban all of those American TV box sets.

'I don't think I've ever been so scared in my life as that,' Fee said. 'But I had to pretend I wasn't scared for Chrissa.'

'You did a brilliant job,' Catriona said. 'You both did.'

'*I* discovered the key was missing,' Brody reminded them.

'You did indeed,' Catriona said, pushing Bagpipe away as his nose tried to make contact with her cookie.

'Is Lexi going to be okay?' Fee asked.

'I think we got to her just in time,' Catriona said, 'but I also think she's got a long way to go to come to terms with how things are now.'

'She told me her mum's living in America,' Fee said. 'She seemed sad about that.'

'That must be difficult for her,' Catriona said.

'But at least she can still visit her mum,' Brody said. 'We can't visit Dad, can we?'

Catriona felt her throat constrict at her son's words but, then smiled as his hand dived into the cookie tin again and took out two more.

'Phew!' he said as he polished the first one off. 'It's been quite a day hasn't it?'

'Yes,' Catriona agreed. 'It has indeed.'

'Girls are much harder work than boys, aren't they, Mum?'

CHAPTER 9

After the drama of the day before, Christmas Eve was a quiet day by comparison.

The MacNeices slept late, breakfasted late and then left the castle, the three of them walking around the grounds together, finding an old walled garden which lay under a light blanket of snow.

'There's not enough to build the world's biggest snowman,' Chrissa said with a little pout.

'But there might be tomorrow,' Iain said. 'I think there's more snow forecast. It's definitely a better option than that hail, isn't it?'

'I hope there's more snow,' she said, her tiny gloved hand swinging in his. 'But just walking's fun too.'

'It is, isn't it?' he said with a laugh and then he instantly felt sad because he simply couldn't remember the last time he'd had a walk with his daughters. Well, other than the disastrous one around the loch which he wasn't going to count. How crazy was it that he didn't have time for such things in his life? What had he been doing for the past few weeks, months, years?

Working too damned hard, a little voice inside him said. *That's* what he'd been doing but that was going to change. He was going to make sure of that.

'Lexi,' he called as his eldest daughter strode out in front of them, her boots making pretty footprints in the snow, 'have you got that camera of yours?'

She nodded. 'Sure,' she said, taking it out of her pocket.

'Shall we take a selfie? Next to that tree there with the red berries.'

They all ran towards the tree and huddled together under its snowy branches. Iain was in the middle, his arms around his girls and Lexi was to his right, stretching her arm out to take the photo.

'Everybody smile,' Iain said.

And they did.

They walked around the loch after lunch and nobody complained that it was too far or too cold and Iain didn't make any unsuitable comments about Lexi's hair and she didn't moan that she wanted to be in California. Somehow he didn't think he'd ever hear her mention

California again, or not in such glowing terms as she once had and, although that made him intensely sad, he couldn't help feeling relieved that his daughters understood what was really going on. They could move forward. They'd always have a relationship with their mother, he knew that, but it would be different now.

'Daddy,' Lexi said that evening. They were sitting by the fire in the living room. Chrissa was sprawled out on the floor with her colouring pens and paper, Iain had been trying to read a Walter Scott novel but was finding it pretty hard going, and Lexi had been staring into the fire for some time now, her ereader forgotten on the sofa beside her.

'What is it?' Iain asked, glad to have an excuse to put Sir Walter Scott down.

'Do you think we can come here again?'

Iain blinked in surprise. In fact, he couldn't have felt more surprised if Father Christmas had plopped down the chimney and danced the Postie's Jig right in front of them.

'You want to come back?'

She nodded. 'Yep.'

'I want to come back too,' Chrissa said, not looking up from her drawing, which was looking suspiciously like Caldoon Castle only a pink and purple version of it.

'Okay,' Iain said, 'I think we can arrange that.'

'Good,' Lexi said and resumed staring at the fire.

Iain picked up the Walter Scott novel again, a little smile tickling the corners of his mouth.

It was strange waking up on Christmas morning in a castle, Iain thought as he got out of bed and drew back the heavy curtains. He gasped as he saw that a fresh layer of snow had fallen in the night. Chrissa would be thrilled and he couldn't wait to see the expression on her face when she saw it. In fact, he was quite surprised that the girls hadn't woken him up already and, after washing and dressing quickly, he went in search of them.

'Chrissa?' he said, knocking lightly on her bedroom door. There was no answer so he opened it a crack. 'Darling?' The room was empty. Maybe she'd nipped into Lexi's.

'Girls?' he called, knocking on Lexi's door and entering but, once again, the room was empty. He looked in the ensuite and the separate bathroom next door and then checked Chrissa's room again. Had they gone downstairs already? They weren't meant to be in the Great Hall yet but maybe curiosity had got the better of them.

He made his way down the stairs, passing the suit of armour and crossing the enormous hallway before checking the living room, dining room and the billiards room. But the girls weren't there.

Panic took hold. Where were they?

He sprinted back up the stairs and made his way down the passageway which led to the Frasers' rooms. He didn't want to disturb them so early on Christmas morning – it wasn't even eight o'clock yet – but he was beginning to feel desperate.

'Hello?' he shouted down the hallway, hoping someone would hear him and that he wouldn't have to knock on any doors.

It was then that he heard voices coming from one of the rooms and he stopped outside a bedroom door which had been left slightly ajar.

'Girls?' he said. 'Are you in there?' He popped his head into the room and saw Lexi, Chrissa, Fee and Brody all gathered around a computer screen.

'Dad!' Lexi said, leaping up from a chair. 'Don't look. *Don't* look!'

'What is it?' he asked.

'None of your business!' she said, pushing him back out of the room.

'I was worried. I couldn't find you.'

'We were here,' she said calmly.

'Well, I know that now,' he said, scratching his head. 'What are you up to?'

'What do you want, Dad?' Lexi asked.

'Merry Christmas to you too!' he said with a laugh and Lexi smiled at him.

'Merry Christmas, Dad.' She stood up on tiptoes and kissed his cheek. 'Now off you go. We'll see you downstairs in a minute, okay?'

Iain shook his head and headed back to his room. Kids, he thought. They really knew how to put you in your place.

Catriona had laid out a scrumptious breakfast of drop scones and maple syrup followed by bacon and eggs and hot chocolate. It was filling but left just enough room to get really hungry for that special meal on Christmas Day, particularly after a walk around the walled garden.

As Iain had predicted, Chrissa was delighted with the snow that had fallen in the night and made several snow angels, had started a snowball fight with him and Lexi and had persuaded them to help her build a snowman. By the time they came in for lunch, they were cold, famished and utterly happy.

After changing their clothes and warming up by the fire in the living room, Iain went in search of the Frasers. He hadn't seen Catriona since breakfast and he hadn't seen Fee or Brody since the strange computer gathering earlier that morning and was missing their company. So, leaving the girls in the living room by the fire, he went to look for them all, finding them in the kitchen.

'Hi,' he said shyly as he entered. 'I didn't mean to disturb you–' he stopped, looking around the kitchen, noticing the sofa strewn with books and games. 'You're living in here?'

Catriona nodded. 'More or less. It's the warmest part of the house,' she said, pointing to the range.

'I had no idea we'd put you out so.'

'But you haven't,' Catriona said. 'We've got the east wing too.'

'But you have a bit,' Brody said. 'We usually use the Great Hall at Christmas.'

'Brody!' Catriona snapped.

'Why then you must join us,' Iain asked.

'Oh, can we, Mum?' Fee said.

'I wouldn't dream of it,' Catriona said. 'We wouldn't want to intrude on your Christmas.'

'But you wouldn't be,' Iain assured her. 'The girls would love to have your company.'

'Muuuuum!' Fee cried. 'Come *on*!'

'Well, if you're absolutely sure?'

'I absolutely am,' he said.

'Great Hall, Great Hall, Great Hall,' Brody began to chant.

'Okay, okay!' Catriona said. 'Let's go.'

CHAPTER 10

Brody tore out of the room followed by Bagpipe who raced through the house with tremendous speed.

'Don't let him near the tree!' Catriona called after them. 'Bagpipe once managed to knock the whole tree down,' she explained to the Iain. 'Lights, baubles, everything. We've got him more under control these days but that enthusiastic tail of his is like an oar of a boat and can do untold damage if left unchecked.'

Collecting Lexi and Chrissa from the living room, the two families made their way through the house until they were standing at the door to the Great Hall.

'This is a special room,' Catriona said as she opened the door and walked inside. 'It used to be the venue for many a grand party where Highland flings would be flung and kilts would swirl around the room.'

'But not anymore?' Iain asked, looking up at the impressive ceiling which, with its numerous beams, looked like an upside down hull of a ship.

'There isn't really much call for that sort of thing now.'

'Have you tried advertising?'

'I've thought about it but I wouldn't know where to begin.'

Iain gave her an enigmatic smile. 'I would,' he said, his glance taking in the fine display of ancient swords above the enormous fireplace in which roared the kind of fire which made you want to settle in for the night and tell stories.

His gaze journeyed around the room, marvelling at the collection of old flags and tapestries which hung down from the massive stone walls and the longest dining table he had ever seen, a small corner of which had been set for his family.

Suddenly, the children were shrieking in delight at the sight of the Christmas tree and there was no chance of having any sort of sensible conversation with that distraction.

Standing in front of an enormous window at the far end of the Great Hall, the tree was over ten feet tall and had been decorated in traditional red, green and gold, with lots of huge tartan bows and ribbons and strings of tiny tin angels and home-made gingerbread biscuits, iced in every colour imaginable, as well as candy canes and foiled-wrapped toffees. It was a feast for the eyes as well as the stomach.

Heaps of presents lay underneath. Catriona had collected the MacNeice's presents the night before from Iain and had placed them under the tree to join her own family's and the result was nothing short of breathtaking.

'Presents after dinner!' Catriona warned. 'And keep Bagpipe away!'

She watched as Brody held on to the deerhound's collar before he managed to find the massive bone that had been wrapped up for him and placed under the tree

The deep stone windowsills around the hall were decorated with great bunches of evergreen and pine cones, which had been sprayed in gold and silver, and three enormous Christmas stockings had been hung to the right of the fireplace. But nothing could rival the tree.

'Wow!' Iain said, giving a long low whistle. 'That tree is something else.'

'It's huuuuuuge!' Chrissa said. Even Lexi looked impressed.

'The Christmas tree is from our own land,' Catriona said. 'Each year we go up the mountain and choose one, don't we?' she said, smiling at Fee and Brody. 'Our neighbour cuts it down for us and brings it in. His fee's a tree for his own family.'

'Nice arrangement,' Iain said. 'It makes our tree at home look like a matchstick.'

'I always say we'll go smaller next year,' Catriona said. 'It takes an age to decorate.'

'Tell me about it!' Fee said. 'We were up on ladders all day and night!'

'And I got spiked about *a hundred* times putting all the gingerbread men on it,' Brody said.

'Well, it looks fantastic,' Iain said.

The two families stood together, gazing up into the tree's deep green depths and sparkling lights, its jewel-bright baubles and glistening tinsel. It was, without a doubt, the most beautiful tree in the world.

'Right!' Catriona said at last, breaking the spell with a clap of her hands. 'Let's get dinner ready.'

'Can we do anything to help?' Lexi asked.

Catriona beamed her a smile. 'I'm sure I can find you all something to do.'

Iain had never enjoyed a Christmas dinner more than the one he shared at Caldoon Castle with his daughters and the Fraser family. The food, which included roast turkey, roast potatoes and parsnips, sprouts, carrots and peas, was all served with tasty gravy and succulent cranberry sauce. The fire behind them roared, Christmas crackers were pulled and stories of Christmases past were exchanged.

'Mom,' Brody began some time after the Christmas pudding had been demolished. 'Mom!'

She didn't reply.

'MUM!'

'Yes? I'm your "Mum",' Catriona said, pronouncing the word correctly. 'Not your *Mom*!'

Brody tutted. '*Can* I tell them my ghost story?'

'I don't think you should,' Catriona said.

'Oh, but ghost stories at Christmas are traditional, aren't they?' Iain said.

'See?' Brody said. 'Go on – let me tell them.'

Catriona sighed. 'As long as it isn't too scary.'

Brody nodded, his eyes shining in glee, and then he began. 'It was a dark–'

'And stormy night,' Lexi interrupted.

Brody glared at her. 'No, actually, it wasn't,' he told her. 'It was dark, yes, but it wasn't stormy. It was calm. Deadly calm. The waters of the loch were still like a mirror.'

'He's good,' Iain said, nodding to Catriona.

'Oh, aye,' she said.

'Stop interrupting!' Brody said, an exaggerated sigh leaving his little body.

'Sorry,' Iain said.

'Sorry,' Catriona echoed.

'The waters of the loch were still like a mirror and the dark red sunset that had come before had looked like blood.'

'I don't like this,' Chrissa said. 'It's too scary.'

Without warning, Brody started screaming. 'Aaarrrghhh!' he cried. 'Aaarrrghhhh! Aaaarrghhh!'

'It isn't *that* scary!' Fee said, watching in amazement as her little brother leapt out of his chair and ran to the far end of the Great Hall.

'What's wrong with him?' Lexi asked. 'Is there a ghost?'

It was then that Iain saw the source of the scream. It was Goliath – the castle's resident spider. But he wasn't just any old spider. He was to the spider world what Bagpipe the deerhound was to the dog world: ginormous. His big dark body looked menacing on eight stilt-like legs. This was a spider that meant business.

Lexi screamed as she saw what both Brody and Iain had spotted and Chrissa and Fee were soon joining in.

Even Iain was on his feet.

'Sheesh, that thing's big!' he cried.

The Great Hall was filled with screams and shrieks as three girls and a boy leapt around, hands flapping in the air as Catriona tried to calm everybody down.

'Get rid of it, Mum!' Fee yelled.

'You know I can't. I've tried before, but he just runs back behind the wood pile. He's a permanent resident, I'm afraid. Look, why don't we all move to the Christmas tree and open the presents? Goliath won't follow us there,' she said.

Everybody moved – fast – to the other side of the room. There weren't many arachnophobes who had the luxury of owning so huge a room as the Great Hall which enabled them to live quite happily in the same space as a massive spider and not notice it.

'Presents!' Brody cried, the spider soon forgotten. There then followed all the fun and frenzy of opening the gifts, with paper and ribbon cascading down to the stone floor as jumpers, scarves, and electronic gadgets and games were revealed to "Oohhs" and "Aahhs".

Catriona watched over the proceedings feeling horribly inadequate as she saw the expensive presents which Lexi and Chrissa were opening compared to the bargain basement items she had bought Fee and Brody. But she need not have worried. Her two seemed absolutely delighted with their gifts and Fee's jumper, which had been lovingly knitted by a friend of Catriona's in Strathcorrie, got some admiring comments from Lexi.

'Dad,' Lexi said, 'we've got a surprise for you.'

'You have?'

Lexi undid the silver locket she was wearing – the one which Iain had bought her in Edinburgh – and he watched as she opened it to reveal a tiny photograph.

'It's the photo we took under the tree in the garden,' he said in surprise. 'How did you do that?'

'Brody did it,' Lexi said. 'He sized it down and printed it out from his computer.'

'That's brilliant!' Iain said. 'Is that what you were all up to this morning at the computer?'

'Yes,' Chrissa said. 'And you nearly spoilt the surprise.'

'I'm sorry,' he said, hugging her to him. 'It's a really lovely surprise too.'

'I've got one as well,' Chrissa said, opening up her own locket to show him.

'I'm going to have to wear a locket myself now,' he said and Chrissa play punched him.

'Can I see it again?' Fee said, coming forward and Lexi handed her the locket. 'It's really lovely. You're lucky to have a father.'

'I know,' Lexi said.

Iain caught Catriona's gaze and could see tears swimming in her eyes as she smiled at him.

He cleared his throat. 'And I've got a surprise for you two,' Iain said.

'More presents?' Chrissa asked.

'Not exactly,' Iain said, looking at his watch. 'Any minute now.'

'What is it?' Lexi asked, looking around the Great Hall as if she might find the answer.

It was then that they heard the distant sound of the phone from the hallway.

'I'll just get that,' Catriona said, breaking into a jog to cover the distance from the Great Hall.

She was back a moment later. 'Girls – it's for you. From California!'

Lexi and Chrissa tore out of the room as Catriona came back in.

'I hope you don't mind,' Iain said once the girls were out of earshot. 'I gave Dawn the number of the castle. The girls haven't been able to get a signal on their phones here and I didn't want them to miss their call.'

'I'm glad she's ringing them on Christmas Day,' Catriona said.

'Me too. You know, she wasn't going to,' Iain confessed.

'Really?' Catriona said, her voice an octave higher than normal with surprise.

Iain nodded. 'She told me when she made the arrangement for me to have them for Christmas. She said – and I quote – "It won't be easy to ring them." Well, after Lexi's episode on the roof, I thought I'd better put her in the picture.'

'How did she take it?'

'She sounded a little anxious, but I could hear a party going on in the background and could tell I didn't have her full attention. Anyway, I made her promise to ring today and I didn't care what she had planned or how difficult it was with the time difference or whose house she was staying in – she was ringing her girls. I told her the time to ring too to make sure we were around.'

'What did she say?'

'I didn't give her a chance to say anything,' he said. 'Except to promise on her life that she would ring.'

'Good for you,' Catriona said.

They watched as Fee and Brody tried to decorate Bagpipe with a piece of tinsel and then Lexi and Chrissa came back into the room.

'Okay?' Iain said.

They both nodded.

'She said she wishes she was here with us,' Lexi said.

'Yeah?'

'But it's okay that she's not,' Lexi said, 'because this has been such a brilliant Christmas!'

CHAPTER 11

The next few days went by in a happy blur of meals, talks and walks. Chrissa was praying daily for heavy snowfall so that they'd get snowed in, because she didn't want to leave, but they all knew that the holiday couldn't go on forever.

'It's going to be really strange going back to Edinburgh,' Iain confessed when it was finally time to leave Caldoon Castle. Their suitcases had been packed and loaded into their car and their final lunch recently devoured. 'The city's going to seem really noisy after this place.'

'Make sure you lock a bit of this Highland silence away for when life gets chaotic,' Catriona said.

'I will,' he said, taking a deep breath of icy air and looking out across the grounds towards the loch in the distance. 'You know, I'd really forgotten how much I love the Highlands, but this trip has brought back so many happy memories and I want to make some of those kind of memories for the girls now. I only hope I'm not too late.'

'Of course you're not too late,' Catriona said and they watched as the four children had a last snowball fight on the lawn.

'Lexi's sixteen now,' he said. 'She'll be wanting to go on one of those awful foreign holidays with her friends soon.'

'Well, let her,' Catriona said, 'but make sure she spends time with you too.'

Iain smiled. 'You're so wise,' he said. 'How did you get to be so wise?'

Catriona shrugged. 'It's not wisdom,' she said. 'It's just survival tactics.'

He laughed. 'You'll have to teach me a few more sometime.'

'It would be my pleasure,' she said.

There was a pause before Iain replied.

'Listen,' he said, 'I'd really love to help you advertise this place. I've got a huge team at my disposal and this sort of project would be right up their street.'

'Well, that's very kind of you, but I don't think I'd be able to afford–'

'You wouldn't need to pay.'

'But I couldn't just–'

'Yes you could. I owe you big time for this Christmas.'

'You don't owe me anything, silly – you've already paid!' Catriona told him.

'You know what I mean. You've played no small role in saving my family,' he said, 'and I'll never be able to thank you enough for that.'

Catriona wasn't sure what to say and so she stood up on tiptoe and kissed his cheek in lieu of any words and couldn't help smiling when she saw a blush colouring his cheeks.

'People need a place like this to escape to,' he said. 'They need to know that places like this still exist. You've no idea how much that's worth to people like me – to know all this is here. To know that *you're* here.'

Catriona pulled her Aran-knit coat close around her and looked back at the place she called home. 'Oh, I think I've got some idea,' she said and Iain smiled warmly at her.

'I'm going to see you again, aren't I?'

'If you'd like to,' she said.

'I would,' he said. 'I really would.'

They exchanged another little smile and then he turned to his daughters.

'Come here, girls!' he shouted. 'I've got something to tell you.' He beckoned them back to him.

'What is it?' Lexi asked, her hair flying back from her face as she ran towards him.

'Tell us, tell us!' Chrissa chimed as she reached him, her soft-gloved hands grabbing hold of his.

Iain put his arms around them both. 'I've made a decision,' he said.

'What decision?' Lexi asked.

'That we're going to live here?' Chrissa asked, her eyes wide with hope.

'No – not quite. But we will be coming back here – I'm sure of that. That is, if you'll have us,' he said, turning to Catriona. 'Because I wouldn't blame you if you never wanted to see us again.'

'Of *course* I want to see you again. *All* of you!' Catriona said with a laugh.

'So, what's this decision then, Dad?' Lexi asked.

'I'm going to work from home two days a week and I'll be going into the office later in the mornings too so we can all have breakfast together. I'm also going to do my best to be around when you come home from school. What do you think of that?'

'You'll *never* do that, Dad. What about your company?' Lexi asked.

'I'm the boss of that company and I can do *exactly* what I want,' he said.

'You're *really* going to do all that?' Chrissa said. 'We'll have breakfast together?'

'We sure will,' he said.

'I don't even know what you like for breakfast,' Lexi said.

'Then you'd better find out because you'll be making it for me,' he said, winking at her.

'Ha ha,' she said, giving him a light-hearted thump.

'Can we get rid of Mrs Crompton?' Chrissa suddenly asked.

'You don't like Mrs Crompton?' Iain asked in surprise.

Chrissa shook her head. 'She's kind of scary.'

Iain frowned. 'Why didn't you tell me this before?' he asked, but he knew why – he hadn't been around for them to tell, had he?

'And she always smells of cabbage,' Chrissa added, making him laugh.

'Well, we can't have that, can we? I think she wants to retire anyway,' he said, 'so let's find someone else, okay?'

'Okay!' Chrissa said.

'Happy?' he asked.

'Happy!' she said.

He turned to Lexi. 'How about you?'

'I'm happy, Dad,' she said. 'Really happy.'

He hugged them both close. 'Time for goodbyes,' he told them and watched as they raced back across the lawn to where Fee and Brody were playing a game of tug of war with Bagpipe. Then he took a big deep breath and sighed it out, catching Catriona's eye.

'It's been–' he began.

'Interesting?' she suggested.

'Well, yes,' he said with a grin.

'You've definitely won the prize for *the* most interesting guests we've ever had.'

'Let's hope you get a stream of really boring ones soon,' he said.

'Yes,' she said, 'I'm not sure we could cope with *too* many interesting ones.'

'The girls have loved it,' he said. 'Especially Lexi. You know – after she got through with hating it.'

'She's a special girl,' Catriona said. 'They both are.'

'I know,' he said, 'and I'm going to make sure I'm around for them. I really am.'

Catriona nodded. 'That's good.'

'Thank you for helping me see that.'

'But I didn't do anything,' she protested.

'Yes you did,' he said, moving an inch closer to her and taking her hands in his, 'and I'll never forget it.'

They stood there in silence in front of the castle, the expression in their eyes understanding one another without the need for words.

'Blimey, it's cold,' Iain said at last, his breath fogging the air.

'Get in the car!' Catriona said, 'before you freeze to death.'

'Okay, okay,' he said, squeezing her hands in his. 'We're leaving,' he called to the girls.

The air filled with a chorus of goodbyes and waving arms and Bagpipe leaped around the snowy lawn, barking at all the excitement.

'Bye!' Iain cried as he got into the car. 'See you soon, okay?'

'Okay!' Catriona yelled back.

'Byeeeee!' the girls cried from the back seat of the car that they were happily sharing.

Fee and Brody waved enthusiastically and then threw a few snowballs at each other before running inside with Bagpipe. Catriona stood there a moment longer, watching as the MacNeice's car bumped down the icy driveway, her vision blurring with happy tears as the car turned a corner and disappeared.

Then, digging her hands deep into her pockets, she turned to head into the castle just as the lightest of snow showers fell from the silver sky.

Christmas at the Cottage

To Roy – remembering Blea Tarn where you held my hand for the first time.

CHAPTER 1

Rachel Myers was the sort of person who always longed for a white Christmas even though the likelihood of getting one was slim. She was one of life's optimists, she just couldn't help it and, as far as she was concerned, all the signs were looking good. For a start, it was the year that summer had never shown up which wasn't surprising where they lived. Her husband Paul would often describe their home town of Carlisle as being "As far north in England as it's possible to get without being in Scotland."

But a dismal summer and a wet autumn made the winter seem unbearably long so the least she deserved was snow for Christmas, she thought as she looked out of their terraced house onto the cobbled street, sighing at the dull grey sky and the constant icy drizzle. The Christmas holidays were just a few days away, but it was far from Christmassy out there.

'That was a very big sigh,' Paul said.

She turned to face him. He was sitting on the edge of the sofa, his floppy fair hair falling over his face as he examined the doorknob which never seemed to stay attached to the door for long.

'I'm sick of seeing streets,' she said. 'I spend all my week staring out of the office at streets and then I come home to more streets.'

'What's wrong with a street?' Paul asked. 'I thought you liked living in town. You said you liked being close to all the shops.'

'But streets aren't fells, are they?' she told him. 'They're not hills or valleys.'

'They're certainly not,' he said, getting up and placing the rebellious doorknob on the coffee table before putting his arms around his wife.

'Maybe we should have found a house in a village. You know one of those pretty Lakeland villages that are all slate and lakeside views?'

Paul shook his head. 'You're not thinking of moving already, are you? We've only been here since the spring. Anyway, you wouldn't have survived the commute for more than a week.'

Rachel sighed again. 'You're probably right,' she said, thinking of the time they'd have had to get up to go to work at the solicitors' where they'd met as graduate trainees. Still, the idea of living in a pretty village appealed strongly to Rachel.

'You're hankering, aren't you?' Paul said.

'What do you mean?'

'I mean, I know what's coming?'

She frowned. 'I don't understand.'

'The cottage. Fell View in the Lakes.'

'What about it?' She turned away from him and stared out of the window again.

'You want to go there, don't you? I can see you're building up to suggesting it.'

'Well, Rowan can't join us for Christmas. She's doing something else, she said. Probably got a new boyfriend. So it wouldn't be a bad idea for us to use the cottage, would it?' Rachel said, cursing how well he knew her. 'It'll just be sitting empty otherwise.'

'You're kidding, right? It would be freezing!'

'No it wouldn't – it would be romantic! Just think – Christmas at the cottage. There's the generator and the log burner and those lovely scratchy blankets you adore.'

He rolled his eyes. 'Don't remind me. If we're going – which I'm not recommending by the way – I'm taking our duvet.'

She laughed at him. 'But you'll love it when we get there, I promise. I'll chop the wood and make the fire.'

He shook his head in mock despair. 'Yeah, right!'

'And make you hot chocolate every night.'

He took a step towards her and looked out onto the street. 'It might be nice to have a change of view for a while,' he admitted.

'So, we're going?' Rachel asked excitedly.

Paul took a deep breath. 'If it makes you happy, we'll go.'

She flung her arms around him and kissed him. 'We could go sledging if it snows,' she said.

'It's not going to snow.'

'You don't know that for sure,' she insisted.

'You're going to be so disappointed if we get there and it's freezing cold and there's nothing but icy, rain-drenched fells to look at.'

She shook her head. 'I'm not going to be disappointed,' she said, 'because it's going to be absolutely perfect.'

Rachel couldn't stop thinking about the cottage now that she knew she was going back there. It seemed an age since she'd last visited. When was it, exactly? It was some time after she and Paul had got engaged. They'd been hiking in Wasdale and she'd taken him up to the cottage to show him. He'd not been as impressed as she'd hoped he would be.

'It's a bit pokey, isn't it?' he'd said.

'What do you mean? It's got three bedrooms!'

'All tiny and –' he'd stopped and sniffed, 'it's a bit musty.'

'Nothing that a few open windows couldn't cure.'

It was a shame they didn't get to use the cottage more often, she thought. It was rented out through an agency during the summer months which meant that Rachel and her sister Rowan couldn't use it then and, once autumn and winter set in, they tended to forget about it which was a shame because autumn could be a magical time in the Lake District with its rich reds, ambers and oranges, and winter frosts turned the valley into a wonderland, crisping the bracken and making the boulders shimmer. Yes, she thought, a trip to Fell View was way overdue.

They had just two more days at work before finishing for Christmas and Rachel couldn't wait to leave her desk. She kept looking out of the window, but it wasn't the rain-drenched streets and the endless stream of traffic she was seeing, but the beautiful blue-green mountains of the west Lake District. The gentle serenity of Buttermere and the majestic grandeur of Wastwater never failed to inspire her. But it was the hidden valley first discovered by her parents which her imagination returned to now.

The old cottage sat at the end of a stony track which wound its way through the hills in an area less frequented by tourists. It had been a place full of adventure when Rachel and Rowan were growing up. They'd filled the valley and woods with shrieks of delight as they'd climbed trees, leapt over rocks and swam in the glacial waters of the tarn. Then teenage years had hit and the girls had been dragged reluctantly to the cottage, bemoaning the distance between them and civilisation. And now? The cottage was a bolthole from reality – a wonderful escape, a place of stillness in an ever-changing world and she couldn't wait to share it with Paul for Christmas.

They left Carlisle on the 23rd of December, travelling down the M6 to Penrith and then wending their way from Keswick to Cockermouth and on down to the wild west of the county to a landscape that boasted England's highest mountain and its deepest lake. They'd done a big shop before their journey. Although Paul insisted that there wouldn't be snow, he was still paranoid about getting trapped at the cottage and so had bought enough food to feed a family of eight, a stack of candles and two extra bags of logs.

As he'd been making sure they didn't freeze or go hungry, Rachel had been making sure that Christmas would be as sparkly as usual with a three-foot Christmas tree in a pot, baubles to decorate it and star-shaped lights to thread around the cottage, as well as the collection of presents she'd been sneakily wrapping for weeks.

As they'd left the city behind them, the sky had turned a peculiar sepia colour and Rachel could see that Paul was worried. Truth be told, so was she, but she didn't dare voice her concerns for fear of Paul calling the whole trip off. The fact was during the summer months, when the sun was shining and the blue skies kissed the mountain tops, the cottage could be a little Eden but, in winter, it was a wild and desolate place.

'This could be a huge mistake,' Paul said as they turned off the road onto the track which would lead them to the cottage. 'If it snows and we get stuck, they could be digging us out dead come spring.'

'Don't be silly,' Rachel said. 'As much as I want it to, it never snows at Christmas except in films and books.'

'I'm just terrified of getting stranded in the middle of nowhere,' Paul said.

'We're not going to get stranded,' she told him, but he didn't look convinced.

It was then that the cottage came into view. White-washed stone with a slate roof and five pretty windows around its front door, it sat snugly in its valley, cosy and inviting.

'Anyway, if we do get stranded, we've got the wood burner,' she continued. 'Just think how cosy we'll be. Just you and me-' she stopped.

'Rach?' Paul said, but he soon realised why Rachel was looking so surprised as he saw the car parked to the side of the cottage. 'Isn't that your sister's car?'

'Yes, it is.'

'What on earth is she doing here?'

Rachel shook her head. 'I have absolutely no idea.'

CHAPTER 2

It was a red-faced Rowan who met them at the door a moment later.

'How did you know I was here?' she asked them, her long dark hair blowing back in the breeze.

'What do you mean? We didn't,' Rachel said.

'Then what are you doing here?'

'We've come to spend Christmas. What do you think we're doing?'

'But *I've* come to spend Christmas here!' Rowan told her.

For a moment, the two sisters just stood staring at each other.

'Look, come in. It's freezing,' Rowan said.

'Well, of course we're coming in,' Rachel said. 'We're not going back now, are we?'

Once everybody was inside and Paul had closed the door on the cold day, the two sisters embraced.

'I can't believe you're here,' Rachel confessed. 'You never use the cottage.'

'Neither do you!' Rowan said.

'And now, here we both are!' Rachel gave a little laugh.

Paul came forward and gave his sister-in-law a kiss on the cheek. 'How are you?'

'I'm good, Paul. You okay?'

'Can't complain. Apart from being absolutely freezing!'

'He's forever complaining about the cold,' Rachel said, rolling her eyes.

'Yes, I've only been here an hour so I haven't got the wood burner going yet.'

'I'll get onto it,' Paul said.

'Which room are you in?' Rachel asked.

'The double – but I can move to one of the twins if you want.'

'Would you mind?' Rachel asked.

'Of course not. I'm just a lowly spinster.'

'Oh, Rowan!'

'I'm joking,' Rowan said quickly as she turned to go upstairs, but there was something in her tone that Rachel caught and couldn't

128

quite work out.

Paul soon came back with a bag of logs and got to work by the wood burner.

'Where's Rowan?' he asked.

'Moving rooms so we can have the double.'

'It won't be the same with her here,' Paul whispered. 'We won't be able to – you know – cuddle up, and I won't be able to walk around in the altogether.'

Rachel giggled. 'Thank goodness!'

'Is she staying?'

'I should think so.'

Paul shook his head.

'What do you expect me to do?' Rachel said. 'Throw her out at Christmas? She's as much right to be here as we do if not more – she got here first.'

'Yes, I did,' Rowan said, causing Rachel to turn around in surprise.

'Ro – we didn't mean-' Rachel sighed, glaring back at her husband as her sister left the room.

'What? I only said-'

Rachel followed her sister through to the kitchen. 'Rowan! Don't be like this. I want you to stay. It's just a bit of a surprise for us both to find you here – that's all.'

'I know when I'm not wanted,' Rowan said.

'You're *very* much wanted so stop being all sulky. Ro? Look at me!'

Rowan turned around.

'Hey,' Rachel said. 'You okay?'

Rowan nodded. 'I'm sorry. I should have checked with you.'

'It's okay. It was a spur of the moment thing. Well, I've been wanting to spend Christmas here for ages, but Paul needed a bit of persuading.'

'I'll get out of your way,' Rowan said. 'You won't want my long face spoiling your Christmas.'

'Don't be silly!' Rachel said, motioning to stop Rowan as she made to leave the room. 'Now, tell me what's going on because *something's* going on, isn't it?'

Rowan sighed. 'I don't know where to begin.'

'The beginning's usually a good place,' Rachel said.

Rowan nodded. 'I've just broken up with somebody.'

'Who?'

'Someone from work at the bank. You don't know him. His name's Chris.'

'How long were you seeing him for?'

'Five months, but I've known him for years. We've always got on well, but he's been involved with someone for ages. Lucy. So I've never thought of him as a potential...' she paused, 'as a potential anything. But then they broke up. The news was all over the bank. Everyone thought they'd be together forever. Chris and Lucy. They were this glorious golden couple. The *perfect* couple.' Rowan sighed.

'So, how did you two end up together?'

'We were on one of those silly training weekends where you have to build a raft and stuff. It was fun, actually. Anyway, I was on Chris's team and we were getting on so well. We'd stay up late at night just talking. He really needed to talk about the whole Lucy thing and he said I was a good listener. I liked listening to him. He was sweet and gentle. There was no bitterness in him about the break-up – just this huge sadness that it had come to an end. And then, somewhere along the line, he stopped talking about Lucy and started talking about me.'

Rachel waited for her sister to continue, not wanting to prod her for fear she might clam up. She had a habit of doing that – giving just a little bit of information and then withdrawing.

'Then he kissed me. It was just a friendly little kiss at first,' Rowan said, smiling as she remembered. 'And then it wasn't.'

Rachel blinked hard. 'It wasn't?'

'It was – you know – a bit more...' she paused as if searching for the right word, 'intense.'

'Got you.'

Rowan walked over to the window, staring out at the misty valley.

'We had five great months together,' she told Rachel. 'I really thought we had a good chance of going the distance.'

'He went back to her, didn't he?' Rachel said, guessing the ending to this particular story and yet dreading hearing it all the same.

Rowan nodded. 'I saw all the signals, but he told me – he told me over and *over* again – that he'd never get back together with her and I believed him.'

Rachel could see tears sparkling in her sister's eyes now and joined her at the window, hugging her close.

'I'm so sorry, sweetie,' she said. 'That's a rotten thing to happen. It really is. You should have called me. Why didn't you call me?'

Rowan gave a big sniff. 'I didn't want to bother you with my problems.'

'But I'm your big sister – that's what I'm here for!'

'I just thought I'd come here to get away from everything.'

'Well, that's what's good about this place – it's certainly away from everything.'

It was typical of Rowan to keep something like this to herself, Rachel thought, to hide herself away with her heartbreak and not want to burden anybody else with it.

'But now I've gone and ruined your time with Paul,' Rowan said.

'You haven't ruined anything,' Rachel promised her. 'We're going to have a brilliant Christmas – the best ever! It'll be just like all those wonderful summer holidays we used to have here only slightly colder.'

Rowan gave a tiny smile. 'Yes, this place was a bit different in the summer, wasn't it?'

'We'll get the wood burner going, go for long bracing walks and cook lots of warming food. Of course, I haven't got you a Christmas present because I didn't know you were going to be here.'

'That's okay,' Rowan said, 'because I haven't got you one either!'

Rachel laughed.

'Are you sure – I mean *really* sure – about me staying?'

'Of course I am, silly! I wouldn't want it any other way!' Rachel said, pulling her sister into a hug.

After a light lunch of soup and baguette, Rachel and Rowan pulled on their boots, coats, hats and scarves and ventured outside, leaving Paul to read the hardback novel his parents had given him last Christmas and which he still hadn't got around to reading.

'You know, I'd forgotten how beautiful this place was,' Rowan said as they headed up the track behind the cottage.

'I hadn't,' Rachel said, 'but I'd forgotten to make time to enjoy it.'

'Both terrible offences,' Rowan said.

'Mum and Dad would be appalled.'

'Yes.'

They walked in silence for a while, each thinking about the parents they'd lost far too early – Mum to cancer and their father to a heart attack. The cottage had been their pride and joy and, however tempting it might have been to sell it for a quick buck, the sisters had instinctively known that it was far more valuable than any price they could have got for it. Even though they rarely got a chance to use it, they knew it was there all the same – a safe and beautiful refuge waiting to welcome them.

They continued up the track, passing through a wood, both knowing where they were heading without the need for words. The Lake District was famous for its enormous lakes, but the majority of tourists never ever found their way to the many beautiful tarns. Rachel was pretty sure that, if you stopped the average tourist in Windermere and asked them what a tarn was, they wouldn't have a clue. But Rachel and Rowan had come to love their very own mountain lake. As tiny as it was compared to the likes of Windermere and Ullswater, it was still enormous to the girls who'd only ever swam in the school pool. And it had belonged to them. Well, it had seemed that way all those summers ago.

Today, great icicles as fat as organ pipes hung from the jut of rock at the far side of the tarn. The bracken was brittle with frost and the boulders sparkled under the faint glances from the sun.

'Remember the summer we swam in there with Michael and Sara?' Rowan said, nodding out to the icy grey water.

'The summer you stole my boyfriend?' Rachel said.

'He wasn't your boyfriend!'

'He would have been if you'd given me a chance to be alone with him.'

Rowan giggled. 'He wanted to be alone with me.'

'Nonsense! You were way too young for him.'

They grinned at each other. If there'd been any bad feeling between them about the summer romance, it had long been forgiven.

'Those were the best summers in the world. We used to have the tarn to ourselves most of the time,' Rachel said.

'Yes. Nobody but us was foolish enough to swim in it.'

'I wouldn't fancy it today!'

'I wouldn't fancy it even if it was the hottest summer day,' Rowan said.

'Wouldn't you?'

'I think there are certain things you leave in your childhood.'

'Do you?' Rachel sounded disappointed.

'You mean, you *would* swim in there?' Rowan said. 'Seriously?'

Rachel looked out across the silver expanse of water and ice.

'Probably not!' They both laughed and then sat in silence for a while on a great boulder as the winter wind pummelled them.

'I thought I'd be married by now,' Rowan suddenly confessed. 'I thought I'd be coming here with my husband and children just as we came with our parents.'

Rachel turned to face her. 'I think you've still got time. You're only twenty-six.'

Rowan shrugged. 'I guess I'm getting bored of waiting. Or jealous of seeing you getting it so right.'

Rachel smiled. 'Hey, I had to wait my time. Don't forget I've got three years of bad dating on you. But I guess I did get lucky meeting Paul. But you'll be lucky too. Just wait and see.'

'I thought I'd got lucky with Chris. You know, I pictured us coming here together. I told him about the cottage and how special it was. I'm glad I didn't bring him here now. I would never have been able to come here again if I had.'

Rachel looked at her sister. 'You've taken a bit of a beating with him, haven't you?'

Rowan sighed deeply. 'I built up all these crazy ideas about our future together. I told myself not to do that, but I couldn't help it. I thought he was the one.'

'But he was Lucy's *one*. Yours is somewhere out there.'

'I sometimes wonder,' Rowan said. 'Maybe I'm destined to be alone. Maybe I should move into the cottage with a horde of cats and learn to knit jam or something.'

Rachel laughed. 'Don't do that! Don't write yourself off. You're just in a fug, that's all. But it'll lift.'

'I hope so,' Rowan said. 'I really do.'

Rachel gave her shoulder a little squeeze. 'Shall we get back?' she said. 'My bum's gone numb with the cold.'

'How did it go?' Paul asked Rachel in the privacy of their bedroom after they'd got back from their walk.

'Well, we talked,' Rachel said. 'She's pretty upset about this guy who broke up with her and I was wondering if any of your friends would be suitable for Rowan.'

'No way!' Paul said. 'Don't even think about matchmaking her with any of my pals. Remember what happened at the wedding with Nick?'

Rachel's eyes widened as she remembered. 'Oh, yeah. I remember.'

'And we thought the two of them would get on so well together. How wrong can you get?'

'Yeah, well maybe if your friend hadn't drunk so much champagne-'

'Don't blame Nick. He'd been having a rough time at work. He needed to cut lose a bit.'

'Not at our wedding, he didn't. And not with my sister.'

Paul shook his head. 'You'll never forgive him for that, will you?'

'Nope!'

'And that's *exactly* why I'd never suggest any of my friends for your sister. You're too demanding, Rachel.'

'No I'm not. You just need to get a better calibre of friend,' she said with a naughty grin.

CHAPTER 3

Nick Madden loved the hills and often wondered how he'd ended up working in London, but the offer of a job at a prestigious advertising company had been too hard to turn down and so he'd left his native Cumbria after graduating and headed south. But oh, how he missed the hills. He'd grown up in a little village near Keswick and would spend every hour he could hiking with his father. They must have clocked up thousands of miles between them over the years, walking in companionable silence with some kind of dog trotting alongside them.

Nick's mother had left the family home two days after Nick's fifth birthday. His father had raised him alone. It hadn't been an easy life, but it had been a pretty good one with the two of them doing all the things that a father and son should do in the great outdoors from camping to climbing, from fishing to rafting. It had been a great childhood even without the presence of his mother. It was one of the reasons it was so hard to see his father as he was now.

Bryan Madden had suffered a stroke three months ago. Luckily, it had been a mild one, but he'd broken his ankle at the same time and his recovery had proved slow. Nick had taken a leave of absence, helping his father as much as he could, but he'd had to return to work and felt quite helpless knowing that his father was on his own. But now that the Christmas holidays were here, Nick was back in the Lake District.

'And he misses you, Harley,' he said now to the ginormous German Shepherd who was walking beside him up the mountain.

Nick stopped to take in the splendour that was Wasdale in winter. The air was crisp and clear, the hills were a silvery-grey and the great lake of Wastwater was almost black in the fading light. It was probably time to head for home and that, tonight, would be the cottage.

When his friend Paul from university had recently lent him a key to his wife's cottage, Nick couldn't believe his luck.

'It's rarely used once the summer's through,' Paul had told him. 'But don't say anything, okay? I'm not sure what Rachel would say.

And tidy up after yourself.'

Nick came down off the mountain, following the track carefully, ice axe in hand. His father had bought him the ice axe for his eighteenth birthday. It had been the best present ever; he couldn't have been more thrilled if he'd been handed the keys to a kingdom because, in a way, he had. Nothing was now unscalable, he'd remembered thinking. No sort of weather could stop him.

Once he was back at his car, he pulled out his phone and tried to get a signal. It was a habit of his to ring his dad once he'd finished a hike, to share the moment. Only there was no signal. Even if there had been, his father probably wouldn't have picked up. Nick had been worried about that. His father was usually very good at responding to things like texts and emails, but that had stopped since the stroke.

'It'll take time for things to get back to normal,' the doctor had told him.

Nick had made sure that his father kept his mobile with him at all times. It was important that he could contact Nick if he needed to. But he never did. It was Nick who did all the running.

He left Wasdale behind him and followed the directions Paul had given him. He wanted to the cottage before dark so he could bring some logs into the house and get the wood burner going. Paul had warned him that the cottage would be freezing.

'This must be it,' he said to Harley as he turned off the road onto a bumpy track that led into the valley. Paul had promised that it was beautiful and he wasn't wrong. With its fields and fells, it was the perfect place to restore the soul after the chaos of life in the city, but there was something else about the place too – a feeling of other-worldliness as if it had taken a step back in time perhaps. It was a landscape he loved and he sorely missed the grey slate cottages, the great scree slopes, the stony footpaths and the soaring fells when he was away from it. But what could he do? His job was in London.

He'd recently been head-hunted by a company that was looking to expand and, when offered the job, had made it a condition that Harley could come to work with him. They hadn't been keen at first but, now, it was hard to imagine the office without Harley's gentle presence. Nick loved it. He loved being able to get up at lunch and venture into the local park for some exercise and air. A London park would never be quite the same as the open spaces of the Lake

District, of course, but he made do. It was why he valued his time in Cumbria so much now, he thought, wishing he could spend more time in the county he'd grown up in. Harley loved it too. He seemed to know that this was his natural environment – that somewhere in the distant past – his ancestors might have roamed these hills and fells.

Nick had read somewhere that domestic dogs were ninety-nine percent wolf and, whilst that was hard to believe of the French bulldogs, pugs and poodles that populated his local park, he could believe it of Harley with his massive paws, his thick pelt and that long, vulpine nose. There was something almost prehistoric about the animal and how he adored him.

The only trouble was, Harley wasn't really his dog.

The sun set early in the valley and it was just beginning to get dark when Rowan let out a weird cry from where she was standing by the living room window.

'What is it?' Rachel said, looking up from where she was sitting on the floor, surrounded by a heap of gold and silver baubles. She'd chosen a place by the wood burner and she was finally nice and toasty and was loath to move.

'Oh, my God! I've just seen a wolf!' Rowan cried.

'*What?*' Rachel said. 'There aren't any wolves in the UK, are there? Not wild ones, anyway.'

'I *swear* that's what I saw. It trotted up the track and went behind the cottage. It was enormous.'

Rachel frowned. It didn't sound very likely. Still, it was as well to take precautions.

'Paul?' she called through to the kitchen where he was making tea.

'What?'

'Rowan just saw a wolf!'

He was in the living room in a flash. 'Is this a joke?'

'Oh, my god!' Rowan exclaimed, keeping up the strange commentary from the window. 'There's a man out there with an axe!'

'Oh, Rowan! This isn't funny. Stop messing around. It'll be dark soon and you're spooking me.'

'I'm serious, Rach. Come and see for yourself.'

Rachel left her baubles and got up from the floor.

'Paul,' she said a moment later, 'there *is* a man out there. *And* a wolf.'

'Oh, you two are the limit,' he said as he joined them by the window.

'Look,' Rowan said, pointing quite unnecessarily at the man whose back was to them.

'Who is he?' Rachel asked, turning to Paul as if he would have the answer.

'Oh, my goodness,' Paul said as he squinted out of the window. 'It's Nick.'

'Nick?' Rachel said.

'Nick Madden – *Nick*.'

'What's *he* doing here?' Rachel asked.

Paul suddenly looked shifty. 'I – erm – lent him a key?' He said it as if he was asking the question of himself.

'You lent him a key? To *our* cottage?'

'Sure, why not? You know he's loves hiking. He said he'd keep an eye on the place if he was ever passing and you know as well as I do that it's hardly ever used out of season.'

'But this is *my* place, Paul. Mine and Rowan's. You should have told me.'

Paul looked suitably guilty. 'Look, I'm sorry I didn't. I just never thought we'd be in this situation.'

They didn't have time to discuss the issue further because it was then that Nick Madden turned around and noticed the three of them looking out of the window directly at him. He waved a gloved hand at them and walked towards the front door.

'Please tell me he isn't staying,' Rowan said, her face now quite pale.

'He isn't staying,' Rachel said.

'He's staying,' Paul countered, moving towards the door and opening it. A moment later and he was backslapping his old friend.

'Nick!' he cried jubilantly.

'Hey, good to see you,' Nick said. 'All of you.' He moved forward and gave Rachel a kiss on the cheek and then nodded to Rowan. Rachel grimaced at the obvious awkwardness between them. She could only hope that Nick wasn't staying for long.

'Come in, mate,' Paul told him, ushering him into the cottage.

'Okay if I bring Harley in?' Nick asked, nodding to the dark hairy beast who was hovering outside.

'Sure,' Paul said. 'The more the merrier.'

Nick whistled and the dog trotted inside, immediately making a beeline for Rowan.

'Oh!' she said in surprise as the big animal shoved its head into her hands.

'He likes a pretty lady,' Nick said. 'Got good taste, our Harley.'

Rachel watched as Rowan blushed.

'He's – er – very friendly,' Rowan said.

'Cup of tea?' Rachel said, remembering to be polite even though Nick was probably the last person she wanted to welcome to the cottage.

'Love one,' he said. 'I finished my flask hours ago. Been hiking in Wasdale.'

'Nice,' Paul said.

'You been up there today?' Nick asked.

'Not for years,' Paul said and Rachel noted a twinge of regret in his voice. She knew that Paul and Nick had been great walking buddies since their university days in Newcastle, but that lifestyle had been left behind once full-time jobs had taken over.

'You should, you know. Beautiful. The light on the water was something else. Had the place to myself for most of the day.'

'I'm not surprised,' Rachel said. 'It's freezing.'

'Not once you've been walking for a few hours,' Nick told her. 'That's one of the things I love about getting up into the mountains. Your whole body seems to turn over. The heart gets pumping and the circulation gets going. I feel like I could run a marathon right now. Although I might just sit down with this promised cup of tea in front of your wood burner if I may.'

'Of course,' Paul said.

'Oh, mind the baubles,' Rachel said, quickly tidying them away before Harley's huge paws trampled on them.

'Sorry,' Nick said. 'He's a little on the big side, isn't he?'

'A *little*?' Rachel cried. 'We thought he was a wolf!'

'They thought you were some kind of mad axe murderer too,' Paul said, earning himself a glare from Rachel.

'What?' Nick said incredulously.

'That axe you were carrying,' Paul said.

'That's my ice axe,' he explained.

'What were you doing swinging it around out there?' Rachel asked.

'I wasn't,' he said. 'I was just going to bring it into the cottage with me to clean.'

'And where is it now?'

'I've left it in the car.'

'Good. I don't really want that thing in here,' she said, as she left the room to help Paul with the tea things. She felt decidedly ruffled by Nick's arrival and was ready to give her husband an earful.

'But I don't see what the problem is,' he whispered, obviously all too aware of his guest in the next room. 'I told him to tidy up after himself if he ever used the cottage.'

'The problem is that we'll all be trapped here together now, and, in case you don't remember, my sister has a problem with your good friend Nick.'

'I know, I know. But it's Christmas so let's all try to get along, shall we?'

'This place just isn't big enough for a six foot four trouble-maker and his wolf of a dog!'

'Of course it is,' Paul said. 'We've each got our own beds. What more do you want?'

'I wanted to be here alone with you,' she said, her voice sounding petulant even to her own ears. 'I wanted it to be just the two of us.'

'I know you did, sweetheart.' He leaned forward and kissed the tip of her nose, 'But we don't always get what we want, do we?'

She frowned at his glib tone. He was enjoying this, wasn't he? He hadn't been at all happy to find Rowan at the cottage on their arrival, but it seemed that everything was hunky dory now that his mate Nick was there.

CHAPTER 4

Deciding that she didn't want to be left alone with Nick in the living room, Rowan went upstairs to her bedroom and closed the door. She couldn't believe what was happening. Nick Madden was here. Not only was he here, but he was going to be sleeping only a stone's throw away from her in the room across the hallway. She took a deep, stilling breath as she tried to calm herself. Nick Madden. Maddening Nick Madden. She'd never told her sister the truth about what had happened at the wedding. She hadn't even really admitted it to herself because it was so awful. But she was going to have to face it now. Just when she thought her Christmas couldn't get any worse. A break-up, her sister and husband muscling in on a holiday she'd so desperately wanted to spend alone, and now Nick turning up to torment her.

For a moment, she wondered if it was too late to leave and return to her home in Penrith, but she knew she'd just brood there. As much as she hated to admit it, it was probably best to have people around her at a time like this, to bring her out of herself, back into the land of the happy, however reluctant she might be to join it. But how was she going to face Nick?

She thought back to the day of Rachel and Paul's wedding. She had been her sister's chief bridesmaid and Nick had been Paul's best man. She and Nick had been forced together in that horribly unnatural way that had crippled her with embarrassment. Nick had been everything she thought she didn't want in a man – loud, over-confident and full of bad jokes. The perfect best man, perhaps, but far from the perfect man. Not like her sweet and gentle Chris.

She shook her head. Her sweet and gentle Chris had proved *far* from perfect, she reminded herself.

Rowan had never been keen on big gatherings and had sneaked away from the dance floor at the earliest opportunity, walking out of the marquee and across the lawn to a terrace overlooking Ullswater. The light was fading in the summer sky and the air was full of swifts and swallows, their high shrieks doing their best to drown out the noise of the wedding party.

'Hi,' a voice had said behind her. She'd turned to see Nick standing there. Now she was female enough to realise that a six foot four guy with dark hair, clear grey eyes and a devilish smile wearing a dapper suit was all too easy to succumb to and he seemed to know the effect he was having on all the ladies at the wedding which annoyed her intensely.

'I've come out to find a space of my own,' she told him, turning back to the lake.

'I came out to find you,' he said.

'Why?' The question was out before she could play the indifference card.

He shrugged. 'I wanted to talk to you,' he said and she noticed that he was holding a glass of champagne in each hand. 'Here.' He offered one to her and she took it, deciding it would be churlish not to.

'You didn't enjoy our dance?' he said.

'I never said that.'

'Not in words perhaps.'

'I don't like being watched by everyone. With them all making assumptions.'

'You mean that the chief bridesmaid and the best man get it together?'

'Exactly,' she said. 'It's embarrassing.'

'I agree.'

'It's a cliché.'

'Yes.'

'And it's never going to happen.' She made the mistake of looking at him then, at his handsome face. Oh, how easy it would have been to have fallen right into that cliché.

It was then that the photographer showed up.

'Ah, there you are!' he said. 'I've been looking for you both. Let's have a little photo of you there. Move in, now. A little closer. That's it. Lovely. Now, how about a little kiss, eh?'

'I don't think so,' Rowan said.

'Oh, go on,' Nick said. 'One for the photo album.' He leaned in towards her and she felt the heat of his mouth on hers before she could protest again and it lasted a little longer than was strictly necessary.

'Got it!' the photographer said, scuttling back to the marquee.

'Wow,' Nick said. 'That was very nice.'

'Forced,' she said, which had been true for the first part of the kiss, but she could have easily ended it. Only she hadn't.

'Perhaps,' Nick said. 'But not wholly unenjoyable, I hope? I mean, with the champagne and the sunset over the lake and everything.'

Rowan hadn't replied. She hadn't trusted herself to.

'I've got to get back.' She slipped away from him and, when she next saw him, it was obvious that he'd downed more champagne.

'Dance with me!' he'd shouted across the dance floor, grabbing her and spinning her around so fast that one of her satin shoes had flown off. He'd skidded across the floor to retrieve it and had tried to cram it back on her foot like a very clumsy sort of Prince Charming. Everyone had laughed and Rowan had been mortified when he'd tried to kiss her again in front of everybody.

That was the Nick Rachel had witnessed with her sister. Rowan hadn't told her about the Nick in the garden who had kissed her so gently with champagne-stained lips and swept her off her satin-wrapped feet under a golden sunset. Rachel had seen the photo which had been taken, of course: it was displayed in her much treasured wedding album, and Rowan had been mercilessly ribbed about it at the time, but her sister had never suspected anything.

Rowan wished she didn't remember it quite as vividly as she did. But she was probably getting herself worked up over nothing. Nick would have had hundreds, thousands – hundreds of thousands of kisses since that evening eighteen months ago. He wouldn't even remember theirs. It was a moment only a silly woman would have locked away in her memory, wasn't it?

Steeling herself because she realised that she couldn't hide in her bedroom forever, she made her way back downstairs to the living room. The curtains had been drawn against the dark now and the wood burner was throwing out its heat. Rachel had put her tiny tree up and it was sparkling with lights and the gold and silver baubles which had been littering the floor when Nick had first arrived. How pretty they looked in the light given off by the fire and the lamps around the room. Rowan remembered that her mother had always detested main lights in a room, preferring the softer glow of a lamp, and Rowan silently threw up a prayer of thanks to her now as she took in the gentle splendour of the simple cottage living room with its beams and beautiful fireplace.

'There you are,' Rachel said from the sofa where she was nursing a cup of tea. 'Can I get you anything? We've all got tea.'

'No, thank you,' Rowan replied, sitting on a chair close to the wood burner. Harley got up from where he'd been sprawling at Nick's feet and settled his huge head on Rowan's lap.

'He likes you,' Nick told her, 'and he's a picky fellow.'

'He just wants to get closer to the heat,' Rowan said.

'He doesn't need to,' Nick said. 'Not with that great coat of his.'

'It is splendid,' Rowan said, letting her fingers stroke the thick fur.

'Hey, Ro, I was just remembering when Nick spun you across the dance floor at our wedding,' Paul said with a laugh.

'Paul!' Rachel admonished. 'I'm sure Rowan doesn't want to be reminded about that.'

'Nick probably doesn't remember,' Rowan said, looking at him for the first time since coming into the room. 'You probably can't remember much about that day, what with all the champagne you drank, can you?'

'I remember enough,' he confessed.

Rowan swallowed hard. 'You remember nearly breaking my toes on the dance floor when you tried to force my shoe back on?'

'You've surely forgiven Nick for that by now, Ro?' Paul said.

'I just want to know if he remembers.'

'I hang my head in shame at the memory,' he said, 'but I'm sure you'll have good memories of that day too?'

'Of course. It was my sister's wedding. I have lots of wonderful memories.'

'Like that sunset over the lake?' Nick asked.

'I didn't see the sunset,' Rachel complained.

'You were too busy slow dancing with me,' Paul said with a wink.

'You get amazing sunsets at this time of year,' Nick said, 'especially up here in the north-west, but nothing I've ever seen has come close to the sunset that evening.' He caught Rowan's eye and she could feel her face flaming. He *did* remember that kiss, didn't he?

'Anyway, as much as I love to reminisce, I think we should get down to practicalities,' Paul said. 'Have we got enough food to see us through? I mean, if there's snow and we get stuck. There's four of us now and we'd better get ourselves organised. It's Christmas Eve tomorrow which means shops shutting early.'

'Darling, you packed enough for the whole county!' Rachel

reminded him.

'Yes, but it's Christmas and we don't want to go without, do we?'

'I've brought plenty of food too,' Rowan said, 'even though I thought it would only be me staying here.'

'I can't bear the thought of you being alone here,' Rachel told her. 'You should have asked to spend Christmas with us.'

'But I am,' she said with a grin.

'Yes, but not by design,' Rachel said.

'What did you bring, Nick?' Rowan asked, acknowledging the fact that she wanted to embarrass him.

He cleared his throat. 'You mean other than a wolf and an axe?' He frowned. 'Not a lot. Enough for a couple of meals for me and the dog.'

'Were you planning on hunting your own Christmas dinner?' Paul said. 'I wouldn't put it past you.'

'No, nothing like that,' Nick said. 'Actually, I was only planning on staying one night. I've got to be somewhere.'

'Sounds enigmatic,' Rachel said.

'Not at all,' he said. 'I'm going to see my dad.'

'How is he?' Paul asked.

'That's what I'm hoping to find out,' Nick replied. 'He doesn't say a lot on the phone and he's terrible at keeping in touch by email since the stroke.'

'Of course,' Paul said. 'I was sorry to hear about that.'

'It must be hard on you living so far away from him,' Rachel said.

'It is. I come up as often as I can, but it preys on my mind all the time. There's also the small problem of Dad not having forgiven me yet, either,' Nick confessed.

'What hasn't he forgiven you for?' Rowan asked.

'Taking Harley from him.'

'He's your dad's dog?' Rachel said.

'Yep,' he said. 'Shortly after his stroke, Dad had an operation on his ankle and there was no way he was going to be able to manage Harley properly so I took him down to London with me. It wasn't ideal, of course. I've got a pretty small flat and had to put him into doggy day care, but he comes with me to work now which is great. But Dad misses him like crazy. I don't think he'll ever forgive me.'

'But it was for his own good,' Rachel told him.

'Yeah, but he doesn't see it that way. I took away his loyal companion.'

They sat quietly for a moment, all eyes on the beautiful Harley who was completely unaware of the trouble he had caused between father and son.

'So you're spending Christmas with your dad?' Paul said.

'I'm leaving first thing tomorrow. Shouldn't be a bad journey to Keswick from here unless it snows, of course,' Nick said.

'If it snows, we'll not allow you to set a foot out of the door,' Rachel said. 'The roads around here would be lethal.'

'I'm making the journey no matter what the weather,' he said. 'I need to be with Dad.'

Rowan looked at the earnest expression on Nick's face and couldn't help admiring his tenacity. Maybe, just maybe, she might have misjudged Nick Madden.

CHAPTER 5

When Rowan awoke, she had that strange discombobulated feeling of not remembering where she was. Her eyes slowly widened and she took in the pale blue painted walls before her and the pretty blue and white curtains at the bedroom window and she remembered. She sat up in bed and immediately shivered. She hoped she wasn't the first up and that somebody had lit the wood burner otherwise she might just go back to bed.

'Coffee!' she said. She'd sneak down to the kitchen to get a cup of coffee. That would warm her up.

Popping a jumper over her pyjamas and stuffing her feet into her fluffy pink slippers, she yawned and opened her bedroom door, checking to see if the coast was clear. It was and so she went downstairs.

She was just pouring the freshly boiled water into her mug when Nick walked into the kitchen with Harley by his side. Rowan was so surprised that she leapt into the air, a splash of hot water scalding her hand from the kettle.

'Ouch!' she cried.

'Hey!' Nick called, flying to her side. 'Cold water – quickly. Get it under the tap.' He grabbed hold of her hand and thrust it under a stream of cold water at the sink. 'How's that?' he asked after a moment. 'Better?'

'Yes. Thank you.'

'Let me see,' he said, examining her hand. 'It's a bit pink, I'm afraid.'

'It's fine.' She withdrew her hand from his, all too aware that the tingling sensation she was feeling couldn't be completely blamed on the cold water.

'I'm sorry I startled you,' he apologised as Harley approached her to say hello.

'I didn't think anyone was up yet,' she said, bending to stroke the dog.

'I'm an early riser. Can't break the habit even if I'm not at work. I've been out for a jog.'

'You like jogging?' she said.

'Yeah. Especially up in the mountains.'

'Me too,' she said.

'You jog?'

'When I can.'

'Hmmmm,' he said. 'I didn't have you down as a jogger.'

'Why not?' she asked defensively.

'I had you down as one of those Zumba women, huffing and puffing in the safety of a village hall.'

Rowan gave a cry of alarm. 'I'll have you know that I've completed a few half marathons in my time.'

'Well, good for you!' he said.

'Yes!' she said and then she frowned. 'Are you teasing me?'

'You're very easy to tease,' he said and she play-thumped his arm. It was then that she remembered she was stood there in her pyjamas with absolutely no make-up on and her hair a fright after a night's sleep. Her hand flew to her hair. 'Erm, I've got to get dressed,' she said, grabbing the half-made cup of coffee and leaving the kitchen.

Nick had seen fewer sights cuter than Rowan Corrigan in her pyjamas and pink fluffy slippers first thing in the morning. She had no idea just how adorable she was, did she? She'd become all self-conscious with her bed-hair and had fled just as things were getting interesting between them.

Nick checked his watch. He wanted to leave for his dad's as early as possible because the weather forecast wasn't good, but he also wanted to spend a bit of time with Paul and Rachel.

And Rowan, a little voice inside him said. *The girl who got away.*

Well, he'd never actually been able to call her his girl so he couldn't really say that she'd got away from him. Theirs had been a strange sort of fleeting nothing, if he was absolutely honest, but it was a fleeting nothing he'd never forgotten.

Over the years, Nick had had a few girlfriends, but he'd never found anyone he felt completely relaxed with. Nobody he could invite for a weekend's hike in the hills, nobody he'd felt connected to.

'You like her too, don't you, boy?' he whispered to Harley who looked up at him with his huge brown eyes.

But he didn't have time to think about how cute Rowan was because he had to get ready to leave. He was becoming increasingly worried about the weather. He popped his head out of the door and looked up into the moody sky full of the threat of snow.

'Nick?'

It was Paul.

'Morning,' Nick said, closing the front door and nodding as Rachel followed Paul into the living room.

'You been out already?' Paul asked.

'Gave Harley a stretch and got some wood in just in case the snow arrives,' Nick said and Paul bent to help him move the wood to the basket near the wood burner.

'Who's for scrambled eggs?' Rachel asked.

'Me!' Paul said.

'Nick?'

'Sounds great. Thanks. You want a hand?'

'No need. This is what I love most about the Christmas holidays,' she said. 'Taking time to make a really hearty breakfast instead of having a rushed bowl of cereal and a measly slice of toast.' She left for the kitchen and, ten minutes later, all four of them were eating breakfast at the kitchen table.

'Look, I can't really delay it any longer,' Nick said as he took a final swig of his coffee.

'But it's madness going out in this!' Rachel said, looking out at the icy sleet that was now hitting the kitchen window at a vicious angle.

'Madness or not, I've got to try.' He got up from the table and went to retrieve his bag from his bedroom.

'The roads will be really dangerous,' Rachel continued, following Nick as he got his things ready. It was then that Rowan came into the room.

'Are you really going?' she asked him. 'It doesn't look safe out there.'

He nodded. 'I'll drive extra slowly.'

'I know I wanted a white Christmas, but I really wish it wasn't going to snow now,' Rachel said.

'You do know it's forecast?' Paul asked Nick.

'Yeah, I heard which is why I'm leaving right away.'

'Well, I'm not going to let you go alone,' Paul said, suddenly grabbing his coat from the back of a chair.

Rachel stared at him in horror. 'What are you doing?'

'I'm going with him. If he gets stuck, he won't be able to get out alone.'

'You're going to leave us here?' Rachel said. 'Seriously?'

'You've got food and heat and each other,' he said. 'You'll be okay.'

Her mouth dropped open. 'But it's Christmas and I want to be with you.'

Paul looked at Nick who shrugged.

'You can all come if you want,' Nick said. 'There's room in the Volvo if you don't mind sharing it with Harley and there's plenty of room at Dad's house.'

Rachel looked at Rowan and the two of them nodded in understanding.

'We're coming with you,' Rachel declared. 'I mean, if that's okay.'

Nick shrugged. 'Fine.'

'Ro,' Rachel said, turning to her sister, 'you don't need to come. Didn't you want Christmas at the cottage by yourself?'

'Not if I'm likely to get snowed in. I don't want to be on my own then,' she said. 'I'm coming with you, okay?'

'Okay, just let me grab a few things,' Rachel added, and the three of them got busy, coming back a few minutes later with overnight bags, several bags of food, a flask of hot tea and a couple of blankets.

They had all just bundled into the car along with Harley and were about to leave when Rachel suddenly yelled, 'Wait a minute!'

'What is it?' Nick asked, eager to make a start, but Rachel had leapt out of the car.

'Rachel? What are you doing?' Paul cried after her. 'We've got to get moving.'

But she'd disappeared back into the cottage.

Nick didn't want to show his impatience at the wife of his friend, but he was beginning to wish he'd sneaked out and taken his chances making the journey alone. He tapped his fingers on the steering wheel and was just about to say something when she reappeared.

'What on earth?' he said.

Paul turned to look at his wife and his face drained of all colour. 'Oh, no! Rachel – take it back.'

She opened the car door.

'I'm bringing the tree,' she told them, doing her best to cram it into the back of the car complete with lights, tinsel and baubles.

'Don't be silly,' Paul said.

'It's only small. It won't take up any room at all. We can't leave Christmas in the cottage, can we?'

Nick looked at Rachel and then at Paul to see if he was going to protest, but he looked thoroughly defeated by Rachel's determination.

'Well,' Nick said as he looked at the two women, the German Shepherd and the Christmas tree in the back, 'you've got to sit with it.'

'And it's fine, isn't it?' Rachel asked Rowan.

Rowan cleared her throat, but didn't say anything.

'Okay, let's get going,' Nick said, looking in his rear view mirror and trying not to chuckle at Rowan who had half a dozen baubles rattling around her face and Harley's head on her lap.

The snow was falling in earnest from the heavens only half an hour after they'd left the cottage. At first it seemed beautiful, something to wonder at and admire, but it soon turned into something sinister, like a thousand swirling demons.

'I've never seen the roads like this before,' Rachel said. 'Do you think we should go back?'

'We're going on,' Nick said. 'That was the plan and you agreed to it when you got in the car.'

'I know,' Rachel said, 'it's just – well – it could be lethal.'

'I feel like I'm in a chapter of The Famous Five,' Rowan said, making Nick chuckle. 'We've even got the dog, haven't we?' she said, giving Harley a cuddle.

They continued driving, slowing the speed right down as they drove through the enchanted white world. On a good day, the journey should have taken them no more than an hour and a half, but it took over four hours to reach Nick's dad's in a village just outside Keswick and they all breathed a sigh of relief when Nick pulled up in the driveway and cut the engine outside an imposing Victorian villa.

'Your Dad still run it as a bed and breakfast?' Paul asked.

'I'm afraid not, and it's much too big for him now, but he refuses to move.'

They all got out of the car, grabbing the bags and the Christmas tree, Harley trotting inside the house with them.

'Are you sure he's home?' Rowan asked. 'There aren't any lights on and it's pretty dark.'

'His bedroom and the kitchen are at the back of the house,' Nick said. 'He's probably in his bedroom. He keeps a plug-in radiator in there as it's easier to warm up.'

Rachel pulled a face as Nick switched some lights on and they walked into a large living room with a big bay window.

'It's very...' she began and then stopped.

'What?' Nick asked.

'Very grey in here, isn't it?'

'I guess Dad never went in for ornaments or pretty knick-knacks.'

'You can tell you grew up without a mother,' Rachel said.

'Rachel!' Rowan cried.

'What? It's true.'

'It's true all right,' Nick said.

'But you didn't need to say it,' Rowan said. 'Anyway, I quite like it. It's very masculine.'

'Oh, you like antlers on the wall and carpets the colour of old socks?' Rachel teased.

'I'm going upstairs. Make yourselves at home, okay?'

Nick left the sisters debating the beauty of grey whilst he took two steps at a time up the stairs, closely followed by Harley.

'Dad?' he called. 'You in there?' He felt ridiculously nervous about finding his father. He'd tried to call him several times to tell him he was on his way up to the Lakes, but he'd always got the answerphone. His dad's neighbour, old Mrs Wray, kept an eye on him and spoilt him rotten with home-baking, he knew. She also had Nick's number in case of emergencies so Nick felt sure that his father was still in good health, but he couldn't help his misgivings as he reached the landing and his father's bedroom door.

'Dad?' he called, softly knocking and entering.

Bryan Madden was sitting in a chair by his plug-in radiator, a thick blanket over his knees. As soon as Harley entered the room, he went and lay down by his master's feet.

'Dad? Are you okay?' Nick was also by his side in an instant.

His father looked up as if confused. 'What are you doing here, son?'

'I've come to see you.'

'What for?'

'What do you mean, *what for*? It's Christmas.'

'Oh, you fool!' his dad said. 'You shouldn't have bothered.'

Nick grinned. It was typical of his father to assume that nobody would bother to visit him at Christmas and, to be honest, Nick hadn't spent many Christmases with his father since getting his job in London, but he'd been worried about him since his stroke and with good cause, he could see now. The place was a mess, it was freezing cold and his father had visibly lost weight.

'Why don't we get you downstairs and light the fire, eh?' Nick suggested. 'The girls will get some dinner on.'

'What girls?' he asked. 'Don't tell me I've got grandchildren you've never told me about!'

'No, you don't need to worry on that score. They're friends. You remember my friend Paul from uni? Well, it's him and his wife, Rachel and her sister Rowan. Come and meet them, Dad. You'll like them.'

'Let me be the judge of that,' Bryan said, getting to his feet.

Nick shook his head. His father gave the impression of being a grouch, but he liked people really. He couldn't have run a successful bed and breakfast for as long as he had without getting on with people.

Nick was relieved to see that his father managed the stairs at a pretty solid pace and they joined the others in the living room where the radiators were just beginning to take the chill off the room and Paul had got a fire going.

'Dad – you remember Paul?'

Paul came forward and shook Bryan's hand. 'Merry Christmas, Mr Madden.'

'Young Paul? Good grief! It's been a few years, hasn't it?'

'It certainly has,' Paul said.

'We've missed you in these parts.'

'Not much time for hill walking these days, I'm afraid.'

'Ah, but you must always *make* time. Don't let work take over,' Bryan said, wagging a finger at him. 'Remember that!'

'I will,' Paul promised and then he motioned to Rachel. 'I'd like to introduce you to my wife. This is Rachel.'

Rachel stepped forward. 'Pleased to meet you, Mr Madden.'

He shook her hand, eyeing her suspiciously.

'I brought our Christmas tree with us,' she said, motioning to the little tree which she'd placed in the corner of the room.

'I don't normally have a tree,' he said.

'No, Dad, you prefer to pretend that Christmas doesn't exist at all, don't you?'

'A lot of nonsense,' Bryan said. 'Just a bunch of sparkling tat!'

Rachel visibly flinched.

'Women like sparkling tat,' Nick said, doing his best to hide a smile. 'Now, let's sit down, shall we? At least it's beginning to warm up in here. You really should put the heating on, Dad. It's the end of December in case you'd forgotten.'

'It's on in my bedroom.'

'But you should heat the whole house.'

'It's too expensive.'

'You've got the money I send you each month,' Nick said.

'I don't want to waste your money, son.'

'It's *our* money. What did you think you were putting me through university for if not so I could help you?'

'You'll need that money for a rainy day.'

'Well, it's a snowy day which is much worse so the heating is staying on. I'll set the timers before I leave and don't you dare tamper with them. I'll send Mrs Wray round to check on you.'

'Oh, that dotty old busybody!'

Nick grinned. 'She's a sweet and caring neighbour and you're lucky to have her.'

It was then that Rowan came into the room carrying a tray with tea things on.

'Who's she?' Bryan asked.

'That's Rowan, Rachel's sister.'

'Rachel's the one who brought the tree?'

'That's right,' Nick said.

'Silly woman,' Bryan said, causing Rachel to blush furiously. 'I like this one. She's nice and practical.'

'Rowan – this is my father,' Nick said as Rowan put the tray down on the coffee table.

'Hello,' she said.

He reached a hand out to shake hers. 'Pretty young thing, aren't you?'

'Dad!'

'What? Isn't a man allowed to say that sort of thing these days?' Bryan Madden shook his head as if in despair. 'What a load of nonsense!'

Rowan gave a tiny smile. 'And you're a very handsome man,' she said.

He barked out a laugh. 'I like her,' he told Nick. 'She's a keeper.'

'Dad, she's just a friend.'

'Yeah? Well, that's your first mistake right there.'

'I'll – erm – just go and find some biscuits,' Rowan said, quickly leaving the room.

'You've embarrassed her now, Dad,' Nick said.

'Oh, rubbish. Women love that sort of attention.'

Nick shook his head and went through to the kitchen where Rowan was searching through the food bags they'd brought with them.

'Hey,' he said. 'You okay?'

'I'm fine,' she said, but she didn't look up.

'I'd like to apologise on behalf of my father.'

'You don't need to do that.'

'He can be a bit full on.'

'I noticed that.'

Nick gave a sigh. 'He's an okay guy, really.'

'You obviously care about him a great deal.'

'I do,' he said. 'I just wish I wasn't so far away in London.'

'That must make life tricky.'

'It does. I'd love to see more of him. Not just to keep an eye on him but, well, we're pals, you know?'

'That's nice,' Rowan said with a smile as she looked up at him.

'Yeah, and I miss that. I miss those times we used to spend together. I mean, we never talked like women do. We wouldn't ever have long, meaningful discussions or anything, but it was nice.'

They held each other's gaze for a moment before Rowan turned back to the bags of groceries.

'Ah,' she said, 'the biscuits.'

Nick opened a cupboard and held out a plate and Rowan placed a handful of chocolate biscuits onto it, her hand brushing his ever so slightly. His breath caught in his throat and he watched for her response, disappointed when her hand darted away from his as if she'd been stung.

'I'll take these through, then,' he told her.

'Yes,' she said, turning her back on him as he left the room.

CHAPTER 6

Rowan wasn't going to think about it. So their fingers had brushed. It had been nothing more than a silly accident – a miscalculation of personal space. That was all. She hadn't felt anything. The sudden surge of warmth around her body probably just meant that the radiators were kicking in. She nodded to herself as she unpacked the groceries, familiarising herself with Bryan Madden's kitchen. It was always good to be practical at times of emotional confusion.

It was a pretty enough kitchen with multi-coloured tiles above a large oven which boded well for Christmas dinner for five, and she smiled when she found a collection of Beatrix Potter mugs in one of the cupboards. All the gang were there from Peter Rabbit and Jemima Puddleduck to Samuel Whiskers and Mrs Tiggywinkle. There were plates to match and Rowan thought that they must be for the younger guests who'd once stayed at the B&B.

'There you are!' Rachel said, coming into the room. 'I thought we'd lost you.'

'No. Just in here,' Rowan said. 'Take a look at these.'

'Oh, sweet!' Rachel exclaimed as she looked into the cupboard. 'Remember when we thought that all the Beatrix Potter characters really lived in the Lake District? We'd poke into bushes and peer into the lakes in search of Benjamin Bunny and Jeremy Fisher?'

'We really did see Squirrel Nutkin that time,' Rowan said, remembering her sighting of the elusive red squirrel.

'But he still had all his tail,' Rachel pointed out.

'Maybe he was a descendent.'

'For sure.'

They laughed and then Rachel looked behind her as if expecting somebody to enter at any moment.

'What is it?' Rowan asked.

'What happened, then?'

'What do you mean? To Squirrel Nutkin?'

'No! I mean Nick came back into the living room all flushed.'

Rowan frowned. 'What's that got to do with anything?'

Rachel shrugged. 'I just wondered what had been going on

156

between you two.'

'Nothing's been *going on*. We were getting the biscuits, that's all!'

'Okay, okay!' Rachel said. 'No need to get all flustered.'

'I'm not all flustered.'

'I was just making sure you were all right. I mean, I know he's not your favourite person on the planet and I know this isn't the kind of Christmas you signed up for.'

'Exactly,' Rowan said. 'I wanted a quiet Christmas so I could get my head around what's been happening lately.'

'I know you did. It's not the Christmas I signed up for either,' Rachel said, her voice now lowered. 'Just look at this place. Isn't it grim?'

'Oh, I don't know,' Rowan said. 'I think it's got an old world charm about it.'

'It gives me the creeps,' Rachel gave a theatrical shiver. 'It's probably haunted or something.'

'It's not that old. It's only Victorian.'

'Are you kidding? *All* the creepiest ghost stories are Victorian.'

'I don't think a bed and breakfast is likely to be haunted,' Rowan said.

'Yeah, well, keep telling yourself that when it starts to get dark!'

But by the time the sun had set and the curtains were drawn, Rachel had made sure that there wasn't a corner of the house that didn't have a lamp on or some form of twinkling lights.

'It's like Blackpool illuminations in here!' Bryan complained. 'It'll cost a fortune in electricity!'

'But it's Christmas Eve, Mr Madden,' Rachel said.

'Yes, and they probably double the cost of electricity at this time of year because of mugs like you.'

'Dad!' Nick cried.

'It's okay, Nick,' Paul said. 'She is a mug.'

Rachel thumped her husband's arm for his disloyalty.

'Well, if we're ramping up the electricity bill, we might as well have the TV on,' Bryan said. There then followed a pleasant enough couple of hours with the five of them watching a Christmas movie, eating nibbles and enjoying light conversation by the warmth of the fire.

After that, Paul and Rachel prepared dinner whilst Nick fed Harley. Everyone was famished after the four hour journey from Fell

View as they'd only snacked on biscuits and cups of tea since then. They ate around a kitchen table and conversation turned to the past with university stories being told to the girls by Nick and Paul and hiking tales being remembered by Bryan. At one point, a look came over Bryan that made Rowan feel intensely sad.

'I'll never get up in the hills again,' he said wistfully.

'Sure you will, Dad,' Nick said. 'You've just got to get your strength back and perhaps wait for a less snowy day.'

That made his father smile a little, but Rowan could see that he had a look of defeat about him.

They returned to their seats in the living room with mugs of hot chocolate. Bryan seemed to have mellowed a little towards his guests by this stage. Perhaps, Rowan thought, he was one of those men who just needed pampering into submission. It must be hard for him living on his own with his only son so far away in London. One was bound to get a bit grumpy especially after not being well.

'Do you miss the bed and breakfast?' Rowan asked Bryan as she sipped her hot chocolate.

'I don't miss the work,' he said, 'but I guess I miss the people.'

'Yeah, Dad might come across as a grouch, but he likes having people around, don't you?'

'Oh, do I indeed?' Bryan said with a guffaw. 'Well, only for short periods of time. That's the nice thing with holidaymakers – they come and then they go. That's good.'

Rowan grinned. 'Well, let's hope we don't all get snowed in until the middle of January.'

'Yes, let's,' Bryan said, and everyone laughed.

They talked for a while more, with Nick and his dad reminiscing about funny guests they'd met over the years, the people who kept in touch and the folks that came back year after year.

'Serious walkers,' Bryan said. 'The coast to coast, the three peaks, the Pennine Way – you name it and they'll have walked it.'

'You'd have loved it in Wasdale yesterday, Dad,' Nick said.

Harley thumped his tail on the floor as if remembering and Bryan nodded and then yawned.

'I think you should probably get to bed,' Nick said.

'Good grief! I'm not a child.'

'Let me help you up.' Nick was on his feet in an instant, bending over his father.

'I can manage,' Bryan said, but it was clear from the struggle he was having to get up from his chair that he needed a little bit of help.

Seeing Nick with his father was a real eye-opener for Rowan. Gone was the brash young man she'd seen at the wedding and in his place stood this caring human being full of vulnerability, and she found herself wanting to reach out and help him.

'Nick?' she asked. 'Is there anything I can do?'

Nick looked around the room as if for inspiration and then looked back at his father. 'A hot water bottle might be nice,' he said. 'You'll find it under the sink in the kitchen.'

'Coming right up,' she said, instantly feeling better at having something to do.

'I don't need a hot water bottle,' Bryan protested and Rowan grinned.

'You'll change your mind when you're all snuggled up in bed with it,' Nick said. 'Come on, let's get you upstairs.'

'I can manage.'

'I know. I'll just walk behind you to make sure you do your teeth.'

'Honest to goodness!' Bryan cried, shaking his head.

'Good night, Mr Madden,' Rachel said.

'Thanks for letting us stay,' Paul added.

'For a couple of nights, tops,' Bryan told them as he left the room.

Paul chuckled. 'You've got it.'

Rowan went to the kitchen and found the hot water bottle and filled it with warm water. Rachel came through from the living room with the mugs and gave them a quick wash.

'Right, we're off to bed,' she said. 'It's been a tiring day. I'll see you in the morning, okay?'

'Which room are you in?'

'Nick said we could have number three – the double with the en suite.'

'He's given me number four – the twin with a view of Derwentwater. If it isn't misty, cloudy or raining.'

Rachel smiled. 'Night,' she said, leaning forward to kiss her sister's cheek.

'Night, Ro!' Paul called from the hallway.

'Night!'

She gave Rachel and Paul a few moments before she went up with the hot water bottle, meeting Nick as he was coming out of his father's bedroom.

'Hey, thanks.' He disappeared inside and Rowan hung around for a moment until he returned.

'Well, I'll get to bed too, I guess. Unless I can get your dad anything else?'

'No, he's good,' Nick said. 'I'm sorry about his brusque manner.'

'I like him,' Rowan said. 'He's honest.'

'Yeah, he's that all right.'

'He's missed you.'

'You think?'

'Of course! The way he was looking at you at dinner.'

'Like how?'

'Like he was trying to capture every single minute with you.'

Nick stared at her and swallowed hard. 'I – well – I've missed him too.'

Rowan nodded and then, after another pause, said, 'Well, I'll get ready for–'

'Hey,' Nick interrupted her. 'There's something I've been meaning to say.'

'Oh?'

He nodded and motioned for her to go downstairs where they could talk without disturbing anyone. As they entered the living room, Nick switched off the main lights so that just the Christmas tree lights were on.

'Doesn't it look pretty?' Rowan said, admiring the way that the silver and gold baubles glowed. 'It reminds of when Rachel and I would sneak downstairs on Christmas Eve and–' she stopped and giggled.

'You didn't open your presents?'

'No!' Rowan said, aghast at his suggestion. 'But we gave them all a pretty good feel. We'd be so excited trying to guess what was inside each one and we wouldn't be able to sleep for hours. Or so we thought. Every year we were determined to stay up and see Father Christmas, but I think we were so exhausted from our excitement that we fell asleep straightaway.'

'And when did you stop believing in Father Christmas?'

She looked thoughtful for a moment, as if trying to see into the past. 'Last year,' she said and then grinned.

'Me too,' Nick said. 'It was hard, but I took it like a man.'

They laughed together.

'Listen,' he said after a moment, suddenly looking uncomfortable.

'What is it? Is it your dad?'

'No, no. It's you.'

'*Me?*'

He shook his head. 'I mean it's me. *You* and me. The wedding.' He sighed and ran a hand through his dark hair. 'I'm not expressing myself properly.'

'You mean Rachel and Paul's wedding?'

'Yes.'

She shook her head. 'We don't need to go there. It was ages ago.'

'I know, and I've never forgotten it,' he said. 'I mean, I don't remember too much about that whole dance floor business, but I'm told that I behaved quite badly and I've carried that around with me ever since.'

'Oh, rubbish! You haven't. You're just saying that because we're stuck together for Christmas.'

'I'm not!' he said. 'I feel bad – really bad – about what happened at the wedding, and I want to apologise.'

'It's okay. You don't need to apologise.'

'Oh, yes I do. If I upset you–'

'You didn't upset me.'

'No? Are you sure about that? Because I've heard differently and you don't seem comfortable around me.'

'You didn't upset me,' she said. 'You annoyed me. You humiliated me. You–'

'Okay, okay,' he said, raising his hands in the air as if in self-defence. 'I get the picture.'

'Let's just forget it, shall we?'

'Are you sure?' he asked. 'Because you still sound upset about it.'

'I'm not,' she said. 'I was mad at the time and, well, for some time afterwards because people kept teasing me.'

'Oh, God – I'm sorry!'

'But it's over. Let's put it behind us, shall we?' Rowan walked over to the dying embers of the fire and knelt down beside it.

'Shall we put another log on?' he asked.

'No. I'm going up to bed in a minute.'

'And you're sure we're good?'

'I've said so.'

He knelt down beside her. 'You know, there's one moment of the wedding that I do remember. Very clearly indeed.'

'Oh?' She didn't dare turn to look at him.

'Yes,' he said. 'Do you remember it too?'

She continued to look into the fire, watching the little orange flicks of flame and the shifting worlds of ash.

'I'm really tired,' she said, getting up from the fire and making to leave the room.

'Rowan?' Nick called after her.

She paused, her hand on the door.

'Thanks,' he said.

'What for?'

'For being so sweet with Dad.'

'You don't need to thank me,' she told him, risking a look at him.

Oh, how she wished she hadn't looked back at him kneeling down by the fireside, his face softly lit by the light from the Christmas tree, his hair flopping over his face and that irrepressible smile of his. She'd refused to talk about her memories of the wedding – that one *very particular memory* of the wedding she'd felt sure he was alluding to – but she couldn't help remembering it.

'Good night, Nick,' she said, quickly leaving the room before her feelings betrayed her.

'Good night, Rowan,' he called after her.

CHAPTER 7

When Rachel woke up on Christmas morning, she peppered her sleeping husband with kisses until he was wide awake too.

'Merry Christmas!' she whispered.

'What time is it?'

'I don't know. But it's light and it's Christmas morning. And it's a white Christmas too. Can you believe it? There's really good thick snow out there. I had a peep before. It's like a scene from a Christmas card.'

He laughed as she got out of bed. 'You're like a big kid,' he told her.

'Come on, let's get up and put the presents under the tree.'

'The midget tree?'

'At least we've got one. There wouldn't be one here at all if we hadn't shown up. Can you imagine? Christmas without a tree and decorations!'

'Outrageous!'

'Yes, it is,' Rachel said, pulling the duvet off her husband in an attempt to get him out of bed. Finally, he complied and the two of them got washed and dressed before leaving their room.

The house was quiet as they sneaked down the stairs like a couple of children in search of presents.

'Where did you leave them?' Paul asked.

'They're in a bag in the kitchen.'

The two of them walked through to the kitchen.

'How's about a coffee first?' Paul suggested.

'No! *Presents* first!'

Paul shook his head, but he was smiling. He knew it was the only day of the year when coffee didn't come first.

They took the heap of presents, that Rachel had carefully packed, into the living room and placed them under the Christmas tree, switching the lights on and admiring the glittering, twinkling scene. Nothing beat a real tree at Christmas no matter how small it was, she thought. Christmas just wouldn't be the same without one and she was so glad she'd brought it with them now, no matter how ridiculous they'd all thought her decision at the time.

Then they started to unwrap their gifts, each taking it in turns to pick one from under the tree.

'Look – it's a cute little bathroom set from Maria.'

'Didn't she give you the same thing last year?'

'I think so, but it's the thought that counts.'

'Shouldn't we wait for the others before opening all these?'

Rachel wrinkled her nose. 'I get the feeling that they aren't into the whole Christmas vibe. I've explained to Ro that I haven't brought her a present as I wasn't expecting to see her, and Bryan and Nick don't strike me as the sort to exchange gifts.'

'Maybe you're right.'

'Rowan was at the cottage to try and forget about Christmas and you've seen what Mr Madden's like,' Rachel went on.

Paul nodded. 'Okay, then, give me my presents!'

Rachel laughed and the two of them set to opening all their gifts.

'Socks from Mum,' Paul said a moment later.

'Good walking socks, though,' Rachel told him, 'and most of your others are horrifically holey.'

'A good excuse to get out walking again. Oh, and a box set of that new drama from Dad. I think he only buys me DVDs he wants to watch. Look – it's been opened already!'

Rachel giggled and then she gasped as she opened a tiny box she'd just unwrapped. 'Paul!'

'Yes?'

'I love it!' She held a little gold necklace up to the light and he leaned forward to kiss her.

'Let me put it on,' he said, taking it from her and placing it around her neck once she'd scooped up her dark hair. 'There.'

She placed her hand over it and smiled at him. 'Thank you.'

Paul opened his present from Rachel next. It was a set of books by Alfred Wainwright, the walker famous for his illustrated guides of the Lake District.

'I knew your old ones were falling apart,' she said.

'They're great,' he said. 'I promise not to drop them into any lakes or off the tops of mountains.'

After finishing unwrapping everything, they collected up all the paper.

'I never want to throw Christmas paper away,' Rachel said. 'I love all the sparkly colours and silly pictures of penguins and Santas.'

'Well, I wouldn't leave anything around for Mr Madden to complain about.'

'Does he really hate Christmas so much?'

Paul shrugged. 'I don't think so. I think he's just a bit tight with his money, that's all.'

'And was he always so rude?'

Paul grinned. 'Kind of. I remember him barking at me when I'd visit in the holidays at uni. I just used to laugh it off. He doesn't mean anything by it. It's just his way.'

'Well, I wish we were at the cottage. Just the two of us.'

'Even without Ro?'

Rachel sighed. 'As much as I love my sister, I wanted it to be just the two of us this Christmas. Is that selfish of me?'

'No,' he said, coming forward and kissing her again. 'Maybe next year will work out better.'

'I hope Rowan isn't too miserable about being here. You know – with Nick.'

'She didn't seem bothered last night.'

'No?'

'They seemed to be getting on okay.'

'Ro's always been a master in diplomacy.'

'Someone mention my name?'

'Rowan!' Rachel cried.

'Merry Christmas.'

They were all exchanging hugs and kisses just as Nick and his father walked into the room, closely followed by Harley who'd obviously spent the night upstairs in somebody's bedroom.

'You lot still here?' Bryan said.

'Merry Christmas, Mr Madden,' Rachel cried, coming forward and giving the old man a kiss on his cheek. He looked startled at first, but then mildly pleased.

Nick laughed. 'You've got red lipstick on you, Dad.'

'Leave it. It might be the last chance I ever get to sport such a souvenir!'

'Well,' Rachel said, 'I think we'd better start thinking about getting the lunch organised.'

Bryan shook his head. 'I don't want anybody fussing around. A sandwich will do me.'

'Nonsense, Dad,' Nick said. 'It's Christmas and I for one don't want to make do with a limp sandwich.'

'And you won't have to,' Paul said. 'We've got enough to feed an army.'

'And I've found the prettiest dining set in the dresser,' Rachel went on. 'Can we use that?'

Bryan looked confused.

'It's white with a pretty red and gold pattern around the rims. Perfect for Christmas.'

'I haven't used that in years,' Bryan said and Rachel saw that Nick was looking uneasy.

'It was Mum's,' he said quietly.

'Oh, well we don't have to use it,' Rachel said.

'No,' Bryan said, 'let's get it out. If you're going to force Christmas on me, let's do it properly.'

Rachel beamed him a smile. 'Great!'

Paul grinned. 'I'd take cover if I was you. Rachel doing Christmas is like nothing else on this planet!'

Paul wasn't joking. After they'd all had breakfast, Rachel gave everyone a job to do from peeling potatoes to finding the most Christmassy music on the radio. No detail was overlooked.

The bed and breakfast dining room which hadn't been used for its true purpose in years and was heaped with junk was emptied of its superfluous contents by Nick. A beautiful red tablecloth was found and Rowan laid the table with the pretty dining set Rachel had found in the dresser before lighting candles.

'They're my power cut candles!' Bryan cried in alarm.

'We'll replace them before we leave,' Nick assured him.

Bryan shook his head, but there was a tiny smile edging its way across his face.

Finally, everything was ready and a slow procession of Christmas food made its way to the dining room table including a big bone which Nick had bought especially for Harley as a Christmas treat.

'Did this all come out of *my* kitchen?' Bryan asked in disbelief as Nick cracked open a bottle of wine.

'Glad you didn't plump for the sandwich option now?' Rachel teased him.

'Well I – I never saw the like!'

'Oh, come on, Dad! We used to celebrate Christmas in style before I moved to London,' Nick said.

'Yes, and that's so long ago, I can hardly remember what a real Christmas is like,' Bryan said and Nick nodded, his eyes taking on a melancholy look.

'Yeah, well that should change from now on,' Nick said. 'Let this be the first of many Christmases to be celebrated in true style!'

'Hear hear!' Paul said, raising his class.

After that, the eating began. Rachel, Paul, Rowan and Nick had all played their part in the kitchen. Even Bryan had pitched in at once stage, topping and tailing the carrots and helping to make the gravy. It was a true feast and Rachel had to admit that she couldn't have enjoyed it more even though she'd previously wished that it was just her and Paul for Christmas.

She looked around the table. She missed a family gathering at Christmas. Rowan had spent one Christmas with her and Paul since they'd got together, but had made excuses the other years, and Paul's parents liked to go abroad for the holidays. So it was wonderful to have a table surrounded by people and she caught Rowan's eye and smiled. Her sister, who was sitting next to Nick on the other side of the table, smiled back. Although Rachel couldn't help but notice that there was definitely some tension between Rowan and Nick. They barely said a word to each other. Had something happened that she wasn't aware of?

After finishing the main course, Rachel insisted on preparing dessert herself, drenching the Christmas pudding in brandy and setting it alight before bringing it to the table. A round of applause greeted her.

'How come you've not found yourself a wife like that?' Bryan asked his son from his place at the head of the table.

'Ah, Paul has all the luck,' Nick said quickly.

'But she's got a sister,' Bryan went on. 'Look! She's right beside you.'

'Dad!'

Rachel saw her sister's face flush in embarrassment.

'What?' his father said. 'Don't you want to meet somebody?'

'This isn't the time or place to discuss it.'

'Well, *don't* you?'

'Yes, of course I do.'

'Then you'd better get a move on,' Bryan said. 'Hey – pretty one. What's her name again?'

'Rowan,' Nick said.

'So you *do* think she's pretty at least?' Bryan said.

'I think you should eat your pudding before it gets cold.'

'The pudding will keep. This won't,' Bryan said. 'Rowan?'

Rachel watched, paralysed by the scene developing before her and feeling helpless to stop it.

'You got a young man?'

Rowan cleared her throat and put her spoon down. 'No.'

'No?'

'I've just broken up with someone,' she said, not looking up from her Christmas pudding.

'Just broken up with someone you say?'

'That's what she said, Dad. Now drop it, eh?'

'Was he blind or something?' Bryan went on undeterred. 'A beauty like you.'

'Dad, please!'

'What? Is it not politically correct to say that anymore?'

'That's right.'

'Well, this is my house. I guess I can say what I like in it.' He gave a little chuckle. 'I haven't offended you, have I, lass?'

'No, no,' Rowan said, but Rachel could see that her sister was feeling distinctly uncomfortable. Her face was still scarlet and she hadn't touched any more of her pudding.

'I – erm – I think I'll go out for a walk,' Rowan announced, suddenly standing up.

'So I *have* offended you?' Bryan said.

'I just need some air now it's stopped snowing,' she explained with a tiny smile. 'I won't be long.'

'Let me come too,' Nick said, getting up. 'Harley could do with a stretch, couldn't you, boy?'

Harley's thick furry tail began to wag in agreement. A walk might just be worth leaving his bone for.

CHAPTER 8

Rowan walked out into the hallway, closely followed by Nick. The two of them put on their coats, hats and boots in silence before opening the door out into the white world.

'Wow! This stuff's quite deep,' Nick said. 'I'd better get the shovel out and clear the path when we get back.'

Harley leaped ahead of them, his thick paws disappearing with each stride.

Rowan and Nick didn't speak for a while, but followed the path down the road, turning off onto a footpath which led into a field. Everything was absolutely pristine. Theirs were the first footprints – and pawprints – across the field and it was so much fun to stride and crunch, leaving three sets of perfect tracks in their wake as they climbed.

A spectacular view of Blencathra, or Saddleback as it was also known because of its fabulous shape, greeted them, its great flanks a perfect white with pale blue pockets defining its shadows.

'Isn't it amazing how snow can change a landscape so quickly?' Rowan said.

Nick nodded. 'Now it all looks like those wonderful Wainwright sketches – everything's black and white.'

Rowan smiled at his reference. It was rare to find a true Cumbrian – especially one who had a great love of the outdoors – who wasn't familiar with Wainwright.

'I – erm...' Nick began, stopping and turning to face her. 'I once again apologise on behalf of my father.'

'You don't need to.'

'Oh yes I do. I'm sorry if he embarrassed you in there.'

'It's fine. He makes me laugh. Well, in a cringey sort of way.'

'It used to be a nightmare taking girlfriends round to meet him. They'd run for the hills as soon as he opened his mouth.'

'I can imagine.'

'It takes someone special to put up with him.' Nick cleared his throat and looked away and they continued walking up the field. Harley bounded ahead of them, barking with joy at the white world and looking particularly wolf-like in the landscape.

'So, what happened?' Nick asked after a moment.

'What do you mean?'

'With the guy you broke up with?'

She looked at him with a frown.

'Sorry. None of my business.'

Rowan dug her hands deeper into her pockets. There was no point in hiding the truth. 'He went back to an ex-girlfriend,' she said.

'What a jerk.'

'My thoughts entirely. So, hence me running away to the cottage for Christmas.'

'I don't blame you,' Nick said. 'The hills are the best place to go when you have things on your mind.'

'And then Rachel and Paul turned up. And then you.'

'Yeah, sorry about that.'

'You seem to spend all your time apologising to me.'

'Sorry.' He smirked. 'And again!'

She laughed.

They walked through a gate in an old stone wall which came out onto a road and it was as they were crossing it that Rowan slipped on the ice. She would have gone crashing to the ground if Nick hadn't sprung forward and caught her.

'Woah there!' he said. 'You okay?'

'Yes, I think so.'

Harley was also by her side, his long face anxious.

'We'd best keep off the roads. The cars have compacted the ice and it's really slippery. Shall we head back into the field?'

'I think we'd better.' They lingered a moment, their eyes meeting and then Rowan broke the spell by taking the dog lead and walking ahead. Harley seemed to be delighted to be back in the field and frolicked around in the snow, making huge circles.

'I've really missed this place,' Nick said, his gaze falling on the village which was far below them now. How pretty it looked with its roofs covered in snow and plumes of smoke coming from the chimneys.

'You ever think about moving back?' Rowan asked.

'All the time,' he said with a sigh. 'Well, since Dad's stroke. Don't get me wrong. London's great. The job's great. But it's a pain I'm so far away. This all feels like another country and I miss it as well as being close to Dad.'

They walked some more, their breath puffing in the icy air.

'Did you ever think about leaving Cumbria?' Nick asked.

Rowan shook her head. 'No, never. This is home. I don't think I could ever leave it. It's the place my parents grew up and their parents before them. It's where Rachel and I played as kids and we've got the cottage too. I wouldn't ever want to be too far from that. It's a wonderful sanctuary.'

'You're lucky.'

'I am?'

'You have no doubts about where you want to be.'

'And you do?'

'All the time. When I was here, I was sure I should be out there,' he said, giving a little nod as if encompassing the whole of the world with it. 'And when I'm out there, I feel I should be here.'

'That's not going to be easy to solve. Unless you clone yourself.'

'Already done that,' he said. 'In fact, *Nick Mark Two* has been absent without leave for some time now. Let me know if you see him, won't you?'

'*Two* Nicks? I'm not sure I could cope with that.'

'Very funny.'

They walked around the field and it wasn't long before they gave in to the temptation to throw a few snowballs at each other, laughing and screaming as Harley bounced around them. They started with small ones, the size of the palms of their hands, but the snowballs got progressively bigger until they were scooping up armfuls of the stuff and flinging it at each other.

'Stop, please stop!' Rowan cried at last.

'Declare me the winner then!'

'Not a chance,' she said, scrunching another handful of snow and pelting him with it.

He laughed. 'Okay. You win. I'm knackered.'

'Lightweight.'

'We'll declare a truce.'

Laughing, they left the field and made their way back home. Nick cleared the doorstep of snow and they both stomped their boots on it.

'Rowan?' he said to her just as she was about to open the front door to go inside.

171

'Yes?'

'I've really enjoyed talking to you.'

She smiled. 'Me too. With you, I mean.'

'Even if you do cheat at snowball fighting.'

'Hah!' she said, play-thumping his arm. 'We'll see about that.'

'Yeah?'

'Yes.'

'Same time tomorrow?'

'If not before.'

'I'll hold you to it.'

The days between Christmas and New Year – those wondrous secretive days where the world seemed hushed and everyone kept to their own little family unit – passed in a blur of eating, drinking and playing. Ancient games from the cupboard in the sitting room were brought out. The chessboard was dusted off, Connect Four matches were set up, there were Scrabble tournaments, card games and a lot of good-tempered arguments over the Hungry Hippos.

It was sometime during this period that Rachel stopped wishing she was alone at the cottage with Paul, and Bryan stopped asking when his guests were leaving. They had become their very own version of a family.

'Dad, have you still got the old sledge?' Nick asked after losing spectacularly at chess to Rachel.

Bryan frowned. 'It's in the shed, I think.'

'Fantastic.'

The sledge, which was a wonderfully old-fashioned one made of wood, was dragged out and dusted off and the five of them, with Harley in tow, took it up to a large sloping field at the end of the village. They weren't the only ones with the same idea because there were families aplenty there, with kids in bobbled hats screaming and valiant parents dragging sledges back to the top again so the whole experience could be repeated over and over again.

'You going to have a go, Dad?' Nick asked.

'It was all I could do to make it to the field,' he said, 'and I'm not risking breaking anything else this year, son.'

Nick nodded. He'd thought his father would say as much and part of him was relieved, but he thought he'd give him the option.

There then followed an hour of chaotic fun as the sledge was shared between Nick, Rowan, Rachel and Paul whose cries of joy mingled with those of the other sledgers. Bryan cheered them on, clapping his hands at their antics and even chucking a few snowballs at them which Harley tried to catch as they hurtled down the hill.

Rowan couldn't remember a time when she'd had more fun. She had all but forgotten her ex and she couldn't help acknowledging the fact that she was becoming rather fond of Nick.

'Your cheeks are all pink!' he said to her as they left the field and walked home.

'Yours are too,' she told him.

'That was fun.'

'Yeah. And to think I was quite happy to spend Christmas on my own. Well, not happy really, but that was my choice.'

'Sometimes, we don't always know what's best for ourselves.'

'Do you feel like that?'

He took a deep breath and exhaled a wonderfully visible plume into the winter air. 'I used to think getting away from this place would be good for me. It has. I mean, I got my degree and my flat and my job and that's all been brilliant. But I definitely left a big piece of me in these hills.'

They looked at each other in understanding.

'Come *on*, you two!' Bryan shouted and Rowan realised that she and Nick had been left behind.

Maybe it was the fact that there was nothing else to do in the middle of a Cumbrian village in winter or maybe it was simply that they actually got on. Whatever the reason, Rowan realised that she liked Nick. She liked walking with him, talking with him, sitting reading a book with him. If she hadn't been forced to spend Christmas with him, she'd never have believed it.

It was she and Nick who took Harley for his walks every day. They were the ones who returned to the snowy field with the sledge when the others made their excuses and stayed inside by the fire. So off they went, pelting each other with as many questions as snowballs and, as New Year approached, Rowan couldn't help feeling deeply unsettled.

'When do you go back to work?' she asked Nick as they were washing up together after tea one evening.

'The third of January,' he said. 'But I'll travel down the day before.

The roads might be bad and it could take me a while.'

'And you're taking Harley?'

'As much as it pains me to, but I don't think Dad's strong enough yet. Especially not walking in all this snow and ice.'

'Harley adores him.'

'Yeah, it's been wonderful seeing the two of them together although, in a way, I wish I hadn't. It's going to make it so much harder parting them. When are you back at work?'

'The second.'

'That's tough.'

'Rachel and Paul too.'

'Work's such a drag.'

She laughed. 'It's what pays for the holidays, though.'

'True and we should start planning the next one. As soon as the snow thaws, I want to get back up here. We could walk around Buttermere together,' he said, 'and Grasmere, ticking off the pretty views, and Friar's Crag on Derwentwater. Did you know Ruskin said it was one of the best views in England?'

'No, I've never heard that,' she said, her mind too fixed on the fact that he was talking about the two of them as a "we".

'Well, we'll start there. Then we'll warm up with Catbells at Easter. Nice and easy. And then Blencathra. Take a picnic to the top and admire the view. Then we'll tackle Striding Edge come the summer.'

Rowan shook her head. 'Oh, no. I'm *not* going over there. I've seen the photos!' She shuddered as she remembered the pictures of the treacherous top and knew that it would really test her skills as a hill walker to get across it. It most certainly wasn't for those who favoured an easy afternoon stroll in the valleys.

Nick put down the tea towel and gave her his full attention. 'But, if we go up Striding Edge, it'll give me an excuse to hold your hand,' he told her.

She looked up into his clear grey eyes. 'You don't need an excuse,' she told him and she felt quite sure that they would have kissed if Paul hadn't come barging into the kitchen wanting to know if there were any dry roasted peanuts left.

CHAPTER 9

It was New Year's Day and it hadn't snowed for a couple of days. The plan was for Nick to drive the others back to the cottage so they could pick up their cars which meant that Rachel, Rowan and Paul had to say their goodbyes to Bryan.

'I'll be back later tonight, Dad, all being well,' Nick told him. 'I'll take Harley so you don't have to worry about him.'

'You take care on those roads,' Bryan said. 'You'll need Harley to keep you warm if you break down.'

'The roads are clear,' Paul told them. 'I've been listening to the traffic news.'

'Good. Good.' Bryan Madden was standing uneasily in the door of the living room. It was Rachel who finally got things moving.

'I'm going to miss you, Mr Madden!' she said, coming forward and flinging her arms around him. 'I never thought I'd say that, but I will!'

'And I you, lass.'

'Really?'

'I think so.'

She laughed as Paul held out his hand to shake Bryan's. 'Good to see you again.'

'You too, lad,' Bryan said. 'Don't be a stranger.'

'I won't.'

And then his attention turned to Rowan who looked as if she didn't quite know what to do. 'Now, I want to see you again too, Rowan. Penrith isn't far. You'll come and visit us, won't you?'

Rowan's anxious face broke into a beautiful smile. 'I'd love to,' she said and Rachel frowned. She knew that Rowan was getting on well with Nick, but hadn't that just been a case of making the most of a bad situation? Rachel had just assumed that this holiday would be the end of her sister having anything to do with the Madden men.

There was slightly more room in the back of the car this time because Rachel had told Bryan that he could keep the Christmas tree and all the decorations as he needed them more than she did and it would give her a good excuse to buy new decorations for next year. But Harley was still sitting between her and Rowan, and Rachel was keeping an eye on her sister, aware of the little looks Nick kept flashing at her in the rear view mirror. She wanted to tell him to keep his eyes on the road which was still pretty treacherous, but she didn't want to interrupt whatever might be going on between the two of them.

Reaching the cottage at lunchtime, they lit the wood burner and cobbled together a quick lunch of soup and bread followed by an every-man-for-himself dive into the tin of chocolates Rachel had brought with them. It was a subdued affair because each of them knew that the end of the holidays was approaching. Nick was heading back as soon as he'd given Harley a stretch and Rowan would be leaving too, driving back to Penrith, whilst Rachel and Paul would spend one last night at Fell View.

After the dishes had been cleared away, Rachel grabbed Rowan and the two of them hid away in the kitchen together. It was the first time they'd been able to talk alone since leaving Keswick.

'It there something you want to tell me?' Rachel asked her sister.

'Like what?'

'Like all the little glances you've been sharing with Nick, and you going back to Keswick to see Mr Madden. Is something going on between you and Nick?'

She watched as Rowan's eyes gazed down to the floor and a dreamy expression crossed her face.

'I think I'm falling in love,' Rowan said at last.

'Who with?'

'Nick, silly!'

'But you *hate* him!'

Rowan shook her head. 'Not really.'

'Good heavens! When did this all happen?'

Rowan shrugged. 'Somewhere between Christmas and New Year.'

'I saw you two were getting pally, but I didn't expect this.'

'Neither did I,' Rowan confessed.

'Why didn't you tell me?'

'Because I wasn't really sure what was happening myself.'

'But he's leaving in a minute. What are you going to do?'

'I don't know.'

'And why you wasting time talking to me?' Rachel said. 'Go on – get outside,' she said, physically pushing her sister out of the kitchen.

Rowan laughed, but she didn't need to be told twice.

'Hey, Rowan!' Nick called as soon as she walked outside the cottage. 'I'm just taking Harley up to the tarn before heading off. Want to join us?'

'Sure,' she said casually even though her heart was thudding in her ears.

The two of them walked side-by-side along the track that led to the wood and up the hill towards the tarn with Harley trotting ahead of them. Rowan was reminded of the first time she'd seen the dog and how she'd thought he was a wolf. How long ago that day seemed now and how much had changed since then.

The snow was still quite thick in places and the tarn was completely frozen over, its surface a glorious silvery-blue. They stood looking out across it and gazing up into the sky which was a startling shade of blue today and looked more like a summer sky than a midwinter one.

'I've been thinking,' Nick said at last.

'Oh?'

'With Dad in Keswick and you in Penrith, I don't think I can ignore the pull of the Lake District any longer.'

'What do you mean?'

'I mean, I need to relocate.'

Rowan frowned. 'But what about your job?'

He gave a shrug. 'Doesn't matter as much as you and Dad.'

Rowan couldn't quite take in what he was saying although his words were exactly what she wanted to hear because she couldn't bear the thought of Nick leaving.

'Nick, are you sure? I mean, you worked hard to get where you are now in your work.'

'But *I'm* not my job. My job's a big part of me, but it's not the most important part. Being here with you and Dad this Christmas has helped me to see that. I want to be here. I *need* to be here.' He looked down into her eyes. 'Rowan – say something.'

'I – I'm anxious. This is a huge decision and we've only just met.'

'I know, but I feel pretty sure about you. I've never felt more sure about anyone in my entire life. And Harley loves you. And Dad likes you too and that's saying something!'

Rowan couldn't help but laugh at that. 'And I really like him and I love Harley.' She bent to stroke the dog's thick soft fur. He'd sat down right between the two of them as if he didn't want to be left out of whatever was going on.

'And me?' Nick said. 'How do you feel about me?'

Rowan took a moment before she answered, thinking about the time they'd spent together over Christmas – the walks and the talks, the snowball fights and the sledging, the little glances they'd shared and the confidences too. There was only one real answer she could give to his question.

'I think I'm falling in love with you,' she whispered.

Nick's hands reached out to cup her face. 'Thank goodness for that,' he said, 'because I think I've been in love with you since our first kiss at the wedding, and I've been dreaming about kissing you again ever since.'

Rowan closed her eyes against the blue of the sky and the white of the snow, feeling all the warmth and love in their kiss. How sweet it was and how wonderfully unexpected to be in the arms of a man she'd once hoped she'd never see again. It was a miracle. Her very own Christmas miracle.

ONE YEAR LATER

When Nick had told Rowan that he'd persuaded Rachel to let them have the cottage for Christmas, Rowan couldn't have been happier. She could think of nothing more romantic than snuggling up to Nick in the cosy little home, and here they were now, cuddling on the sofa with Harley at their feet and a fire blazing in the wood burner.

There were Christmas decorations all around the cottage's living room. A red berry wreath hung on the back of the old wooden door and strings of fairy lights shone along the dark beams. Tea lights flickered along the mantelpiece and a huge bunch of mistletoe had been tied to a hook in the beam. There was also a little Christmas tree in the corner of the room decorated in red and gold baubles and old-fashioned children's toys made out wood and painted in brilliant primary colours. Rowan had insisted on having a tree. Of course, there was a full-sized one at Bryan's house in Keswick where they'd be spending Christmas Day. Rachel and Paul were joining them there too – at Bryan's invitation.

'Might as well have the lot of you,' he'd said, a tiny smile tickling the edges of his mouth.

Rowan was really looking forward to Christmas Day at Bryan's again. Nick was living there now. He was managing a new branch of s company in Carlisle and business was good and he'd told Rowan that his time in London was done although he had the occasional trip to the capital to touch base with head office. And how much fun had they had since he'd moved back to Cumbria in the spring? They'd done all the walks they'd talked about including a hike across Striding Edge where Nick had kept his promise to hold Rowan's hand every step of the way. Bryan had even joined them on a couple of the easier walks around Ullswater and Buttermere as his ankle was now completely healed.

'I've got a lot of catching up to do,' he'd told them both.

Nick had been thrilled to see his father out in the hills he loved so much.

'Fancy a walk?' Nick asked Rowan now. Harley's tail immediately started thumping.

'I've just got nice and warm by the fire,' Rowan said.

'I'll keep you warm,' Nick said with a grin. 'Don't you worry about that.'

She smiled right back at him.

They pulled on their thick winter coats and boots before leaving the cottage. The ground was iron-hard under their feet with patches of ice all around. It was a good excuse to hold hands. Not that they needed an excuse these days.

Instinctively, they made their way towards the tarn. It was their special place. Was there a more beautiful place in the world, Rowan wondered? There might be warmer places, sunnier places, drier places, but there probably wasn't a more beautiful one.

Rowan often wondered where she'd be now if she hadn't decided to spend Christmas at the cottage last year. She certainly wouldn't have been here with Nick now, would she?

'You don't regret leaving your job and your life in London, do you?' she asked him as they walked around the tarn, a shaft of sunlight turning the ice into a sparkling wonderland.

'Not for a single minute,' he said, stopping to kiss her.

Rowan still hadn't told Rachel about that first wonderful kiss she and Nick had shared at the wedding. She'd decided not to. That kiss was her and Nick's little secret — a secret she hoped to repeat over and over again for the rest of her life.

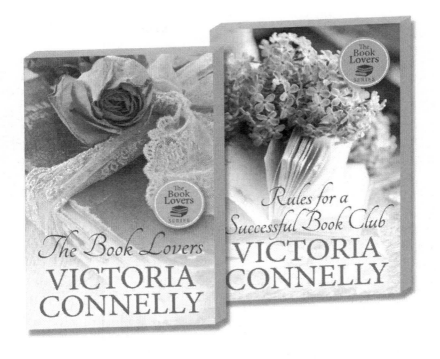

The Book Lovers series – out now

Ebook Paperback Audio

ABOUT THE AUTHOR

Victoria Connelly was brought up in Norfolk and studied English Literature at Worcester University before becoming a teacher. After getting married in a medieval castle in the Yorkshire Dales and living in London for eleven years, she moved to rural Suffolk where she lives with her artist husband and a Springer spaniel and ex-battery hens.

Her first novel, *Flights of Angels*, was published in Germany and made into a film. Victoria and her husband flew out to Berlin to see it being filmed and got to be extras in it. Several of her novels have been Kindle bestsellers.

To hear about future releases sign up for Victoria's newsletter at: www.victoriaconnelly.com

She's also on Facebook and Twitter @VictoriaDarcy

BOOKS BY VICTORIA CONNELLY

The Book Lovers series
The Book Lovers
Rules for a Successful Book Club

Austen Addicts Series
A Weekend with Mr Darcy
The Perfect Hero
published in the US as Dreaming of Mr Darcy
Mr Darcy Forever
Christmas with Mr Darcy
Happy Birthday, Mr Darcy
At Home with Mr Darcy

Other Fiction
The Rose Girls
The Secret of You
A Summer to Remember
Wish You Were Here
The Runaway Actress
Molly's Millions
Flights of Angels
Irresistible You
Three Graces
It's Magic (A compilation volume: Flights of Angels,
Irresistible You and Three Graces)
Christmas at the Cove
Christmas at the Castle
Christmas at the Cottage
A Dog Called Hope
The Full Brontë

63392034R00115

Made in the USA
Charleston, SC
03 November 2016